D0829082

continued . . .

"If you are even a casual fan of figure skating, you will love this book. The author . . . really knows the behind-the-scenes dish . . . The character of Bex is one of the best amateur sleuths to come along in some time . . . The mystery is interesting, and the investigation is so entertaining that you'll be glad you're along for the ride. I'm already impatiently awaiting the next book in this series."

—*The Romance Reader's Connection*

"Adams uses her extensive knowledge of the real-life world of competitive figure skating to create a very realistic background for this murder—and possible blackmail—mystery complete with hints of dark humor. A likable, down-to-earth heroine makes this a must-read for cozy mystery fans with a fascination for figure skating."

—*Romantic Times*

"Adams's style is light and breezy, and the book moves right along. She wickedly portrays the behind-the-scenes backbiting and jealousies of television personalities, both on- and off-screen. Readers who enjoy a lighter mystery and those who are intrigued with the rumored infighting in the world of competition figure skating should enjoy this one!"

—*Books 'n' Bytes*

"*Murder on Ice* mirrors events from the last Winter Olympics. Corrupt judging, cutthroat battles between the skaters, and the behind-the-scenes viewpoint all help to add depth to this unique mystery . . . This marks the first book in the new Figure Skating Mystery series. It is shaping up to be an addicting collection of books." —*Roundtable Reviews*

Berkley Prime Crime titles by Alina Adams

MURDER ON ICE
ON THIN ICE
AXEL OF EVIL

Axel of Evil

ALINA ADAMS

BERKLEY PRIME CRIME, NEW YORK

THE BERKLEY PUBLISHING GROUP
Published by the Penguin Group
Penguin Group (USA) Inc.
375 Hudson Street, New York, New York 10014, USA
Penguin Group (Canada), 90 Eglinton Avenue East, Suite 700, Toronto, Ontario M4P 2Y3, Canada
(a division of Pearson Penguin Canada Inc.)
Penguin Books Ltd., 80 Strand, London WC2R 0RL, England
Penguin Group Ireland, 25 St. Stephen's Green, Dublin 2, Ireland (a division of Penguin Books Ltd.)
Penguin Group (Australia), 250 Camberwell Road, Camberwell, Victoria 3124, Australia
(a division of Pearson Australia Group Pty. Ltd.)
Penguin Books India Pvt. Ltd., 11 Community Centre, Panchsheel Park, New Delhi — 110 017, India
Penguin Group (NZ), Cnr. Airborne and Rosedale Roads, Albany, Auckland 1310, New Zealand
(a division of Pearson New Zealand Ltd.)
Penguin Books (South Africa) (Pty.) Ltd., 24 Sturdee Avenue, Rosebank, Johannesburg 2196, South Africa

Penguin Books Ltd., Registered Offices: 80 Strand, London WC2R 0RL, England

This is a work of fiction. Names, characters, places, and incidents either are the product of the author's imagination or are used fictitiously, and any resemblance to actual persons, living or dead, business establishments, events, or locales is entirely coincidental. The publisher does not have any control over and does not assume any responsibility for author or third-party websites or their content.

AXEL OF EVIL

A Berkley Prime Crime Book / published by arrangement with the author

PRINTING HISTORY
Berkley Prime Crime mass-market edition / January 2006

Copyright © 2006 by Alina Sivorinovsky.
Cover illustration by Teresa Fasolino.
Cover design by Lesley Worrell.
Interior text design by Kristin del Rosario.

ISBN: 0-425-20685-8

BERKLEY® PRIME CRIME
Berkley Prime Crime Books are published by The Berkley Publishing Group,
a division of Penguin Group (USA) Inc.,
375 Hudson Street, New York, New York 10014.
The name BERKLEY PRIME CRIME and the BERKLEY PRIME CRIME design are trademarks belonging to Penguin Group (USA) Inc.

PRINTED IN THE UNITED STATES OF AMERICA

10 9 8 7 6 5 4 3 2 1

Prologue

Figure skating champion Igor Marchenko twice made the front page of the *New York Times*.

The first time, in 1977, he was fourteen years old, a green stalk of a boy wearing an oversized down jacket and ill-fitting boots stained with gray Moscow slush, nervously running his hands through fine ash blond hair that looked like it had been chopped by the same blind barber who used to hack at Prince Valiant. His freshly bruised eyes looked as though he were afraid to take in the full consequences of what he'd just done. But, at the same time, his lips were set in the firm determination of a man twice his age, ready to take responsibility for his actions.

At the height of the U.S.–U.S.S.R. Cold War, the all-capital letter headline above his slightly out of focus, black and white Associated Press wire photo triumphantly taunted: "DEFECTING!"

No one could blame them for the big type. It was a superb story, thoroughly worthy of braggadocio coverage, even by a newspaper as traditionally averse to headline-blaring yellow journalism as the *Times*. For, even as Moscow played host to the 1977 World Figure Skating Championships, the Russian Men's Bronze Medalist had ducked his KGB guards and snuck out of the athletes' hotel, braving subzero temperatures to cross several blizzard-ravaged miles on foot in the middle of the night. He arrived at the American embassy hours before it opened and buried himself in the snow beneath a pair of bushes by the front gates to avoid being seen by passersby. He huddled there, shivering to near convulsions, until sunup, when he was finally able to stumble inside the embassy, and, teeth chattering beneath frozen black and blue lips, a Russian accent fighting for authority over a cracking, adolescent tenor, he blurted out, "I defect."

The Soviet Skating Federation, naturally, put up an invasion-force-sized clamor, claiming that the boy had been coerced, bribed, kidnapped, and any other relevant term they could coax out of their handy Russian/English dictionaries. But, Igor, with a poise and calm utterly unexpected of a one-hundred-and-twenty-pound ninth-grader, remained firm in his convictions. The only time he came even close to wavering was when the president of the skating federation dragged Igor's mother, older sister, and brother-in-law to the sidewalk outside the U.S. embassy, where Igor could clearly see them from the window. The federation head handed the American ambassador a note to pass on to the boy. It read, "You will never, ever see them again."

Igor came to the window, and he stared at his family. His mother was crying. His sister was crying. Igor was crying. But, after a tense, hour-long standoff, he simply turned around and walked away.

Eventually, the Soviets gave up. They had to. Young Igor certainly showed no signs of doing so. And, after nearly a month of high-pressure tactics, they allowed their top male skater to be taken to the United States.

There, he received the hero's welcome traditionally reserved for World Series champions, astronauts, and Girl Scouts who have sold the most cookies. He met with the president. He chatted with Johnny Carson on *The Tonight Show*. (Well, technically, Johnny chatted with Ed McMahon about how wild and wacky it was that male skaters wore all those sequins on their costumes and they did those jumps where they spun round and round—how did they keep from feeling dizzy or getting a sequin in their eye?—while Igor sort of nodded politely, smiled, waved at the camera, and looked desperate to defect again, this time from Burbank.)

Donations poured in from well-wishers eager to help the young hero continue his skating career in the U.S.A. The United States Figure Skating Association (USFSA) gave him free room and board at their Olympic training center in Hartford, Connecticut, and pressured their congressman to rush through Igor's citizenship papers so that he could represent the U.S. at the 1982 Olympics. Actually, they were really hoping that he could represent them in 1978, but that, the congressman told the USFSA, was really pushing things. U.S. citizenship usually took seven years to finalize. The right word to the right people might be able to speed up some paperwork and make it five years, but a single year was out of the question. As a result, even though Igor won the 1978 U.S. National Championships (with so many 6.0's one newspaper compared him to Damian, the boy with the 666 tattooed into his skull from the then-hit movie, *The Omen*), it was the runner-up and 1977 champion, one Gary Gold, who went to the 1978 Olympics and finished in seventh place, very respectable for a seventeen year old at his first Games. But, not nearly as respectable as the silver medal Igor won at the World Championships a month later. (He would have won Gold, USFSA officials insisted publicly, if those crooked Russian judges hadn't all ganged up with the Polish, Czech, and East Germans against him. How typical.)

Four years later, Igor did win Gold, not just at the Worlds, but at the Olympics, as well. This time, however, his exploits weren't earth-shattering enough to merit the front page of the *Times*. Sure, it was a gold medal won for the U.S., their single one of those entire Games, but, it was only in figure skating, after all. Not in a real sport, like, oh, say, golf.

And so, Igor had to wait over a quarter of a century to get his second front-page news story.

In the meantime, he retired from amateur competition, skated professionally for a few years, then became a coach at the same Olympic training center that had once taken him in.

"To pay back a debt," he explained.

"Aw . . ." everyone thought.

And, in the end, it was his coaching success that, in December of 2005, brought a now forty-two-year-old Igor Marchenko back to Russia for the first time since his chilly desertion.

Igor's top student, 2005 U.S. Ladies' Silver Medalist, Jordan Ares, had been invited, along with her teammate, 2005 U.S. Ladies' Bronze Medalist Lian Reilly—Gary Gold's top student—to skate in a "U.S. vs. Russia" made-for-TV event in Moscow.

At first, Igor refused to attend. Exactly the same way he'd refused to attend any other competition held on Soviet soil while he was an amateur, and on formerly Soviet soil once he was a coach. It wasn't until the Russian Figure Skating Federation's president personally issued an invitation, a sort of "Come home, all is forgiven; Love & Kisses, Russia— P.S. We'll even let you see your family again, isn't that terribly nice of us?" missive, that Igor agreed to the trip.

This news made the 24/7 Sports Television Network very, very happy. Sure, it was in their contract to cover the event anyway, but now, on top of the up-close-and-personal profiles they were planning to tell all along—Lian vs. Jordan, their final head-to-head before the 2006 Nationals, where, due to the retirement of Erin Simpson, the 2005 champion, the U.S. ladies crown was at stake, and during an Olympic year to boot—now, they actually had a naturally (as opposed to a manufactured) dramatic story to tell: "Igor Marchenko Comes Home for the First Time." Oh, this was going to be a tearjerker, they could just feel it. The producers were already debating whether to use the Beatles's "Back in the U.S.S.R." or John Denver's "Take Me Home" for the primary background music. (Although everyone agreed that Neil Diamond's "Coming to America" should definitely be played when they recapped the part about his dramatic escape. That one was a gimme.)

Fortunately for the gag reflex of the viewing public, neither ditty came to be. On the day of the first practice in Russia for the American girls and their coaches, Igor Marchenko collapsed in Natzionalnaya Arena. He was dead before the ambulance got there—three and a half hours after it was called.

"Of course, Americans would get the most prompt service," the arena manager, whom everyone seemed to simply call Shura, groused in Russian. "Special privileges only for Americans."

Lying facedown and inert barely three feet away from the ice surface upon which his star-making competitive career first began, Igor Marchenko finally earned his second *New York Times* story.

This time, the headline read: "MURDERED!"

One

"Well, Bex, looks like you did it, again," Gil Cahill, executive producer of the 24/7 network's broadcast of "U.S. vs. Russia: A Figure Skating Challenge," announced during their first production meeting at seven A.M. sharp in the hotel's conference room the next morning. "You've gone and gotten us another skater killed."

Bex winced and thought Gil was really stretching it. Was it her fault it just so happened that, at last year's World Championships, the Italian judge who everyone felt unfairly handed the ladies' title to Russia's dour Xenia Trubin instead of America's pert Erin Simpson, had found herself unfortunately electrocuted and that Bex ended up solving the crime? And was it her fault that, a few months later, a teenage skater Bex had urged 24/7 to profile for the upcoming U.S. Championship ended up kidnapped, with murder and mayhem to follow, and Bex had been forced to solve that case, too? (Well, actually, the latter kidnapping/murder, etc., had sort of been her fault to begin with; but that is too long a story to dissect in detail at this juncture.) The fact was this time she hadn't been in the country at the time the murder occurred, so she'd had nothing, even peripherally, to do with Igor Marchenko's death. And Gil had no right teasing her like he had.

He also, it seemed to Bex, had no right to follow up his jolly accusation with the following: "So, I figure that means you owe us another brilliant solution."

Okay. Now she felt certain he wasn't just teasing, but mocking her.

Despite having one full year of 24/7 service under her belt, Bex was, nevertheless, the newest full-time staff member in the room, as well as the youngest, a fact not looked too kindly upon by those veterans who'd done the math and were distraught to calculate that they were old enough to be her parents.

"Are you paying attention to me, Bex Levy?" Gil picked up his research binder, the one weighing three pounds, seven ounces. Bex knew the exact weight because she was the one who'd photocopied every single page, punched the holes, and slipped them into Gil's binder after he insisted he couldn't be bothered with such administrative work. Gil picked up his three-pound-plus research binder, and after raising it over his head, dropped it down on the desk. The clatter it made was inversely proportional to how early it was, and how little sleep everybody had gotten the night before (two hours and forty-seven minutes, assuming they fell unconscious the minute their heads hit their pillows and that they weren't bothered by the housecoat-clad old-woman floor-matron walking up and down the hall, berating the bellboy at the top of her lungs for not being quiet enough).

Ergo, the clatter of binder hitting table was very, very loud.

Everyone in the production meeting jumped to attention. They were all shocked. But not surprised. Gil did his binder trick at least three times a meeting. He thought it kept his people sharp and inspired them to concentrate. Personally, Bex thought it made them all wound-up and incapable of thoroughly focusing on any one thing since a part of their frazzled psyches was on perpetual binder alert, but what did she know? This was only her second season as a researcher, whereas Gil had been an executive producer at 24/7 since cavemen had used bones for skate blades.

On the other hand, for the sake of accuracy—as a researcher Bex was nothing if not a slave to accuracy—she did feel obligated to point out, at least to herself, that there was another reason besides jet lag and a seven A.M. sharp command performance time for why so many were so often so inattentive at a Gil Cahill meeting: they were boring.

Not that Gil wasn't an interesting speaker. Well, he actually wasn't, but he'd begun his broadcasting career as an announcer, so even when he had nothing germane to say, he said it in a pleasant and melodious manner. (Besides, a man who could at any time send a binder flying at the desk, or worse, at your head, deserved to be described by a plethora of words, of which "interesting" would definitely have to be included.) The boredom came from the fact that Gil insisted on having his below-the-line meeting at the same time as his above-the-line. He insisted that the tech people, like the cameramen, the soundmen, the assistant directors (ADs), and the videotape operators, who were primarily concerned with how the show looked and sounded from a technical point of view, be in the same room for the same meeting as the story-driven people—the writer, the feature producer, and the researcher, who were primarily concerned with what skaters were to be featured during the broadcast, and how they would go about spinning their tales from a narrative point of view. This meant that, in any Gil Cahill meeting, at least fifty percent of the people in attendance were hearing a discussion of issues that were utterly irrelevant to their jobs. Under such circumstances, the mind did have a nasty tendency to wander.

"I am paying attention to you, Gil," Bex tiredly insisted.

What did the man expect? The entire crew had just flown in the night before from New York. A ten-hour airplane flight, followed by the delight that was Russian customs. (Were those people banished to Siberia for answering a question directly, and did they get their food rations based on how many hours they kept foreigners waiting in line, trying to juggle their luggage in one hand, their passports in another?) Of course, for Bex, that particular period of joy was followed by a tête-à-tête with the Russian police department, because Gil insisted he absolutely needed to have Bex's write-up of all the known information on the Marchenko murder prior to her going to bed. So, instead of squeezing in an extra hour of sleep alongside her lucky-bastard colleagues who got to go straight to the hotel, Bex spent a precious sixty minutes at a Russian police station, playing charades in her attempt to wheedle out what they knew about Igor Marchenko's death.

To be fair, fifty-six minutes of that time had gone to finding out who the correct person to bribe for the information was. Once she learned that, the rest was a snap.

Her bribee was so generous, he even kindly offered to translate the Russian police report and transcribe it into English for her—for a small extra fee, naturally. The last minutes of her excursion were spent listening to him explain how it was doubtful the case would ever be solved. Russia these days bred crime, both the organized and disorganized kind, he explained, faster than it did alcoholics. They were very understaffed. Some of the officers hadn't been paid in weeks. No one was exactly motivated to investigate the death of a lucky Russian son-of-a-bitch who'd been ingenious enough to get out in time and make his fortune in America, because, to be truthful—how you say this in English?—nobody gave a damn.

Yet, to Gil Cahill, it didn't matter what kind of night Bex or the rest of the crew had already endured. Production meetings were always, always, always held at seven A.M. local time. Gil said it gave them a head start on their day.

So here they were, twenty-four tired people seated around an oval table in a Moscow conference room with no windows, and a map on the wall so old (or in denial) that it still showed the Soviet Union as controlling its wayward republics. And Poland. And Alaska.

At the center of the table stood a platinum pitcher of brown liquid that tasted like leftover water someone had rinsed a handful of old coffee beans in. Their catered continental breakfast consisted of smoked halibut, fried pork chops, and sour cherries in a sugary, watery paste. At seven A.M., Bex was having trouble deciding which delicacy she found least offensive.

Since this was their first meeting of the event, along with the below-the-line and above-the-line troops, the Talent had also been commanded to make an appearance. The Talent, or, to put it more accurately, the on-air announcers for "U.S. vs. Russia" were Francis and Diana Howarth. The American husband-and-wife team were Olympic Pair Champions in 1962 and 1966. As far as Bex could tell, their final Split-Twist-Lift was the last time they'd agreed on anything. Fortunately for their three children, Francis Jr., Diana Jr., and Frances Dyana, their parents considerately saved up all of their at-home arguments so that they might have them live on the air during skating broadcasts. Right now, however, even they were too tired to do more than quibble about their introductory copy—should it be, "Hello, I'm Francis Howarth, live from Moscow with my lovely wife, Diana." or, "Hello, I'm Diana Howarth, live from Moscow with my husband, Francis, the jackass."?—before glazing over and dozing off.

This early in the day, the only non-jet-lagged people in the room were the four "runners," kids hired locally to serve as gophers and translators for the production. They didn't get to sit around the table. They stood with their backs against the wall, looking simultaneously eager to please and extraordinarily confused. Bex's assigned runner was a young man who resembled an eager fourteen-year-old starting his first day of big-boy school. His brown corduroy pants were rolled up at the ankles, showing a pair of black socks. His sports jacket, while technically still qualifying for inclusion in the brown family, nevertheless missed matching the pants by a mile. He wore a yellow tie on top of a collarless shirt. The entire ensemble looked as if it had been handed down by an older, much more broad-shouldered cousin. And yet, despite the assortment of fashion faux pas, Bex's assistant for the next week, Alexander "Sasha" Serota, had greeted Bex with a firm, confident handshake and, in admirably competent English, informed her, "I would like to learn much everything about the television production, so that I may soon become Ted Turner of Russia."

To Sasha's credit, his dazzling self-confidence did not flag an iota even as Gil began his precision binder-hurling exhibition. Whenever Bex turned around to look at him, Sasha flashed her a brilliant smile that seemed to say, "Americans are insane, especially that one throwing binders around, but I am sure you are not like them in the least and will straighten everything out for me shortly."

Well, at least one person had confidence in Bex. Although, based on Gil's earlier challenge, she guessed she ought to amend that to two people. In either case, she hadn't the slightest idea why.

"Gil." Bex forced her sleep-deprived brain to form a thought: noun, verb, noun, verb, suppressed expletive. "Did you just say you expect me to solve Igor Marchenko's murder?"

"You have to," Gil spoke in his patented, Al-Gore-to-slow-school-children tone. "We've already promoted it on the air. See, Bex, last night, as soon as I read your report saying that the police had determined that Marchenko was murdered with some sort of heart-attack-inducing drug—"

"It was a homeopathic version of digitalis. The killer poured it into Marchenko's gloves and left them on the radiator to dry. A few minutes after Marchenko put them on, he was poisoned by the topical contact of such a large dose."

"Right, whatever. Anyway, as soon as I read it was murder and not just a boring heart attack, I got on the phone to New York and told them to start heavily promoting that we would be solving the murder, live, on the air, during the ladies' long program. They were nuts about the idea. We got some terrific buzz when we solved that Silvana Potenza thing on the air last year."

"*We* did?" Bex wanted to ask, but didn't. "*We* solved the case, did *we*?"

"Problem was, last year, we couldn't promote the big reveal in advance. You really dropped the ball on that one, by the way, Bex."

"Gil, if that hadn't worked out according to plan, we would have looked like the biggest idiots—"

"Still, I'm willing to overlook it. Fresh season, fresh slate and all that, right? But, I am also not going to make the same mistake twice; that would be stupid. So this time, we are going to promote the hell out of this thing. I'm having them satellite us the promo spots as soon as they're done so we can take a look. This is going to be huge. We're all counting on you. Don't let us down."

"Gil, are you mental?" is what Bex should have asked. If she weren't a gutless weenie who really, really couldn't afford to lose this job.

The root of the problem was that Bex grew up a latchkey kid. Which meant she watched an inordinate amount of television. Which meant she had programmed her brain to receive massive amounts of information at an abnormally high speed. Which meant that, by the time she was in her teens, she'd become an information junkie. The Internet becoming big around that time didn't exactly help. By the time she'd started college, Bex had no one particular interest. She was

simply obsessed with learning everything about everything.
Which was why she couldn't settle on a major, and ended up
going to Sarah Lawrence where they were above such
things. Which was why she had no applicable job skills. Except for gathering, absorbing, documenting, and disseminat-
ing information. And so, here she was, the proud possessor
of one of those rare research jobs that hundreds of other college-
graduate generalists were probably dying to step over her
corpse to get.

Which was why, instead of proposing the obvious, "Are
you mental?" question, Bex instead pointed out, "But, this
isn't like Silvana, Gil. I was at least around when the Silvana
murder happened. I knew the people involved. I knew who
had a grudge against her, and why. I knew where everyone
was at the time of the murder because I was there, too. I
don't know anything about what went on at the arena yesterday. I wasn't even in the country then."

"Not a problem." Gil never thought anything was a problem, as long as he could delegate the work necessary to confirm his point. "They're having a press conference at the
arena first thing this morning for all the media. They'll catch
you up. It's supposed to be starting any minute. In fact, Bex,
I'm surprised. Why aren't you over there already, getting us
the best seat in the house?"

Somehow, contrary to the laws of physics as understood
by average humans in the twenty-first century, Gil always
expected Bex to be in several places simultaneously. At a
competition, if the men were practicing in one arena, and the
women at another, Gil never seemed able to understand why,
at the end of the day, Bex could only turn in one practice report. He would look at her carefully typed sheet, genuinely
puzzled each and every time at receiving only half the expected write-up. Then he would sigh deeply to express his
immense disappointment with the shoddy job she was
doing. After the sigh, he would always advise Bex to work
harder.

Heck, who knew, maybe Gil was right? Maybe if Bex just put in a little more effort on top of the eighteen-hour days she usually put in, she just might very well unearth the secret to time travel. Anything was possible, after all.

As for why she wasn't already over at the arena, getting 24/7 the best seat in the house, well. . . . "Maybe it's because I'm over here, Gil, getting binders flung at me," Bex didn't say as surely as she hadn't offered her host of other rejoinders earlier.

Instead, overwhelmed by the sheer denseness of the man, all Bex could say was, "So, I just need to go to a quick press conference and I should be able to solve this murder, too? Any suggestions on how exactly I'm supposed to do that?"

"Figure it out." Gil shrugged, seemingly unconcerned either by her assignment, or by the pressing, looming imminence of her four-days-from-now-ladies'-long-program deadline. "You're the researcher."

"Researchers? They solve crime? This is what the researchers do?" Bex had to hand it to Sasha. The young man had actually waited politely for the meeting with Gil to end. He had waited for Bex to come up to him, make small talk, and for the two of them to walk out of the hotel and hop into the rickety cab heading for the Natzionalnaya Arena, where the competition was scheduled to take place over the next four days, before Sasha, politely but with unabashed curiosity, posed his question.

If Bex were in his shoes, she suspected she'd have pounced with a query before the meeting was even over. But, then again, Sasha was presumably a well-brought-up young man, whereas Bex was an "I-got-to-know-it" fiend.

"No." She chose her words with great precision, allowing most of the fury she was currently feeling towards Gil to spill out and drench Sasha. And the cab. And the streets of this dingy city.

This was Bex's first visit to Russia. A lifetime of reading everything from *Dr. Zhivago* to Stolichnaya Vodka ads had prepped her to expect a glistening, snow-covered winter wonderland. A cross between *Swan Lake* and a festively painted Fabergé egg. In actuality, winter in Moscow meant gray, unwashed sidewalks beneath gray, unwashed buildings, and cold, angry people rushing about with grim, gray expressions, dressed in gray, washed-out clothes, oppressed on either side by a gray, perpetually cloud-filled sky. Instead of *Swan Lake*, Bex felt like she had fallen into used dishwater.

"No," she told Sasha with a weary sigh that encompassed both her disappointment with the city and over ever having been born. "Researchers do not, as a rule, run around solving crimes. We leave that to professionals. Like ex-sitcom stars turned MD's. And little old ladies living in Maine. And bored rich people."

Sasha's blank expression quickly told Bex that the unfortunate young man had never seen so much as a single episode of *Diagnosis: Murder*, *Murder, She Wrote*, or *Hart to Hart*. Which was a pity, really. Because, right now, that meant Bex was the only one with crime-solving experience. Which, despite her earlier success with the Silvana Potenza murder and the Jeremy Hunt kidnapping, still consisted primarily of watching all of the above.

"I see." Sasha nodded in all seriousness. "Then please to tell me, what is it that the researchers do?"

"Well, you know that binder Gil smacked on the table earlier?"

"I—Yes . . ." Sasha's voice trailed off uncertainly, as if he feared Bex doing a reenactment of that maneuver with the identical binder that she now balanced on her lap.

"That's the research binder for this competition." Bex moved to open it. Sasha flinched.

"It's alright," Bex reassured. "It's not loaded."

Again, Sasha stared at her blankly.

"Right, never mind." Bex made a mental note to herself. She had to remember she wasn't really as funny as she thought she was. She should just stick to facts. There was less trouble to be gotten into that way.

"This binder is where we keep all our research material for any one particular show. I put it together and I made copies for everyone so that we're all on the same page once we get here."

Bex figured that eager-eyed, enthusiastic, as-yet-unjaded Ted Turner–wannabe Sasha didn't need to know that it felt like more than three-quarters of Bex's day was spent in front of a copy machine in the most remote room of 24/7's New York headquarters, feeding thick reams of paper through the photocopier and praying for it not to jam. The remaining one-fourth of her day was spent un-jamming the copier, trying to figure out which pages in the cycle had actually gotten done and which ones hadn't, reorganizing the remaining pages, prying staples out with her teeth, restapling and, finally, washing the black ink off her clothes. Television was very glamorous work.

"You see, right here." Bex indicated the first four pages up front, under the heading, HISTORY. "This is background on Moscow, on Russia, on all the competitions that have been held in this arena."

"This will be on show?"

"Maybe." Bex sighed, loathe to admit the other reality that drove her crazy about her job. Which was that, of the roughly two hundred pages of research she generated for each event, odds were that only point one of one percent of it would be used. The fact of the matter was that the scintillating information detailing how Moscow wasn't always Russia's capital (it was actually moved several times under the Czars and the Communists) did not bear much relevance on how many triple jumps Jordan Ares or Lian Reilly landed in their Long Programs, or whether either girl cheated on her Lutz jump by changing her blade's edge at the last minute and turning it into a Flip, or, more colloquially, a Flutz. But the fact remained that sometimes the historical information did come in handy. For instance, Bex could only imagine the havoc it would engender if, in the middle of a broadcast, Francis Howarth got it into his head to announce that the height of one of the competitors was exactly equal to the region's annual rainfall. And woe be it to Bex if, at that moment, she was unable to produce a document confirming that obscure fact, on the fly.

Which was why, no matter where they were headed, be it Moscow or Paris or Geneva or even New Jersey, Bex dutifully wrote up her historical facts and the major import/export data, all the while knowing full well that, odds on favorite, nobody would give a damn.

Depressed by that always most depressing of things, truth, Bex hurried to change the subject, thumbing through the pages until she got to the few that she knew would be read. She showed Sasha. "Here, we have the skater's element sheets. Right here we write down the name of their music for both their Short Program and their Long Program, plus all the elements in the order they are planning to do them. See, it says Lian Reilly, and there's the pronunciation, *Lee-ah-nn*, so the announcers say it right, and then her music for the short program, *Carmen* by Bizet, a most original choice—"

"You are being funny, yes?" Sasha asked.

"I am being funny, yes," Bex reassured herself to see that the runner had a sense of humor. It would serve him well in the days of production ahead and quite possibly be the only thing capable of retaining Bex's sanity once Gil fully stretched into his, "Come on, people, we're putting on a show, here," mode. "Anyway, Lian's music is the ever popular *Carmen*, and her elements are . . . I put them in order so the announcers could just follow along down the list . . . first a double Axel, then a Layback Spin, then a footwork sequence—"

"Why is it," Sasha asked, "that you need to write this down? Do the people who make talking during the program, can they not see what performers are doing on the ice?"

"That would require lifting their heads from the binders," Bex explained. "See, these sheets, originally, they weren't for the announcers, they were for the tape-operators in the truck. Strange as it may seem, your average tape-operator does not know a triple Salchow from a triple Axel, so that during a live broadcast when Gil is screaming for an instant-replay, "Rewind the tape back to the triple Axel, now, now, now!" they have no glimmer what he's talking about. By listing the elements in order like this, Gil can just scream, "Rewind to element number four!"

"Now, now, now?"

"Oh, yes, that's part of the routine; and they can just go to element number four. The problem is, when the announcers found out about these sheets, they demanded them, too. Now, they're like addicts, they're totally hooked. Why look at the program when you can just read off your cheat sheets? So we go to the skaters, and we ask them to list their elements for us. The problem is, you end up with stuff like this: See here? Lian's combination jump is listed as a triple Lutz/triple Toe Loop, which, by the way, she has yet to ever, ever land in competition, but she insists she's going to do it, so I keep putting it down, idiot that I am, and every time she chickens out and goes for the triple/double, Francis and Diana glare at me, like it's my fault. But . . ." Bex smiled at Sasha. "I digress."

Sasha smiled back. "Is okay. I like."

"Good, because there'll be a lot more of that." Bex pointed to the page facing the one with the skater's elements. "And then this is their biography. See, we've got Lian's name again, and her pronunciation, *again*, because Diana doesn't like to look from one sheet to the other, she says it confuses her. And here we have Lian's bio information. Her name means 'my joy,' and her mother named her this because she'd been trying to have a baby for five years, and then trying to adopt for ten, and nothing was working, and then, finally, when she was forty, she and her husband adopted Lian from China."

Sasha tapped the bio sheet as if uncovering the answer to his question was the same as coaxing a goldfish to the corner of its bowl. "You know all this news of her?"

"It's my job to know all this news about her. That's what a researcher does. Fortunately, in the case of Lian, it isn't that difficult. Her mother is what we, in America, like to refer to as a motormouth. You ask her, 'How are you?' and you get a lecture on what joy her joy, Lian, has brought her today. You so much as nod politely in her direction, and she corners you for a forty-five minute discussion the theme of which can best be described as, 'So, tell me, what do you love best about my precious Lian?' "

Understanding dawned in Sasha's eyes. That look of faith he'd radiated in Bex's direction during Gil's meeting came back with a vengeance. "That is why Mr. Cahill puts you in charge."

"Oh, no, no. I'm not in charge. I'm pretty much the lowest person on the totem poll when it comes to the show."

"But, no. I hear him. He puts you in charge of finding out who killed the poor man, Marchenko. He put you in charge because you know everything about everyone."

On most occasions, Bex would have appreciated the compliment. On most occasions, she liked to think that she did know everything about everyone. Not only because it was her job, but because she prided herself on being one of those people who actually listened. She prided herself on being able to absorb facts other people might miss, and use them to draw conclusions other people might overlook. Boy, but she was an arrogant little snot, wasn't she?

Well, in that case, she'd gotten no less than what she deserved. You're so smart, Bex, then solve another murder, why don't you? And this time, just to knock it up a notch, do it in a foreign country where you don't speak the language. And do it in four days. That shouldn't be too difficult for a clever girl like you, right?

"I—" Fortunately, the sentence Bex had no idea how to end got lost in the screech of the taxi's tires as it pulled up to the front door of the arena. Bex and Sasha exchanged looks. The young man watched Bex for guidance and a hint as to what he should do.

Figuring that there really was no choice in the matter, Bex gestured for Sasha to climb out of the cab. She, reluctantly, did the same. They walked towards the arena.

And into a madhouse.

Two

Apparently, in the twenty-four hours since Igor Marchenko slipped on his poisoned gloves and fell to the floor in a deadly convulsion, the world had discovered non-Olympic figure skating. From the one local, Moscow reporter who'd shown up the day before to write a feature on how present-day Russians were too busy struggling to give two blini about art, culture, or sport, the press corps had swelled to include representatives of every Moscow-based American television station, several American newspapers and radio stations, plus members of the French, German, British, Dutch, and even Greek fourth estate. The press conference room was packed. A babel of the inquisitive tossed their bulky, winter coats atop the few available gray folding chairs, then balanced precariously on the tottering two-tier structures as they thrust forward red-light-blinking tape-recorders, or clutched spiral notebooks with stiff, chilled fingers. Those unable to get a seat leaned against the wall and made up for their distance from the podium by simply shouting their questions, regardless of whether or not they'd been called on.

At the microphone stood Penelope Fuki, newly-elected president of the United States Figure Skating Association. She'd worked her way up to the leadership position after spending almost seventeen years on the finance committee. While other officers—athlete's advisory, singles and pairs, dance, grievance, rules, ethics—argued and battled and plotted and backstabbed and lobbied to get their way asap, Penelope sat quietly in the back and balanced the budget. She spoke only when spoken to, smiled at anyone who asked a question, and never missed a deadline or a decimal point. As a result, when it came mandatory time to elect a new president, Penelope was the only member of the USFSA who hadn't offended or made enemies out of seventy-five percent of the voting body. And so she became president. A week before boarding the plane for Moscow and the "U.S. vs. Russia" match. The press conference following Marchenko's death was the first one she'd given, ever. When Bex and Sasha arrived, it was not going well.

Penelope stood at her podium, shrieking in decibels usually reserved for dog whistles and Celine Dion concerts. For those who'd never heard her utter a word, this was the first surprise. The second was that the woman who for years had diligently tracked every expense, every receipt, every donation from conception to rubber-stamp, seemed incapable of doing the same thing with a thought. Now, granted, it was hard to know which question to answer when the entire international press corps was lobbing them at you, theater-in-the-round style, in a half-dozen languages. But, even when Penelope did manage to pluck a single query out of the fracas and attempt to respond to it, she very quickly skidded off-track.

"Penelope! Penelope! Over here! Does the USFSA take any responsibility for Marchenko's murder?"

"Will the competition be cancelled, Penelope?"

"Do you trust the Russian authorities to conduct a fair investigation, considering Marchenko's status as a notorious defector?"

Penelope waved her arms in front of her chest, fingers splayed, palms flapping back and forth at the wrist, as if her answer was bubbling its way up from her rib cage to her neck, throat, and finally mouth. "The USFSA deeply regrets Igor Marchenko's death. Naturally, we expect all aspects to be looked into when trying to figure out what exactly happened to him and who may be responsible, but, the fact is, it would do Igor no good for us to cancel a competition that was months in the planning and has already been purchased for TV broadcast rights, which is a very difficult proposition in today's harsh financial climate but people forget that it's our primary source of funding, funding that goes to young athletes for development and holding local competitions which are not televised but are critically important, especially for the boys in our sport, an area where we also have a critical deficit, which is why we can't come close to competing with the rest of the world on the Pairs and Dance field, which is why there is no Pairs or Dance in this competition, and why no men, although our American men are quite good, there is no doubt about that, but until we remove the social stigma—"

She went on in a similar vein for another fifteen minutes. When it looked like the vein was about to become a major artery, Bex tried to decide if Penelope was actually extremely clever and simply choosing to masterfully obfuscate the issue at hand until every single reporter grew frustrated and left, or whether she genuinely was that bad at this whole press conference thing. If it were the former, Penelope could definitely put a checkmark in the "mission accomplished" column. Right around the time she started rhapsodizing about the beauty of Moscow, three-quarters of the press picked up their coats and slunk out, figuring they had a better shot at getting their questions answered by Shura, the grumpy custodian, than by the woman in charge.

Luckily, none of the aforementioned press had to sink quite that low since, in addition to the rather ineffective press conference, there was, simultaneously, a practice session going on at the ice surface a few feet from the meeting room.

Bex and Sasha followed the rest of the throng into the tunnel that led to the main arena and to the ice. The six-thousand-seater was eerily quiet so early in the day. The sound of flashing and scraping blades echoed off the empty, metal seats, and a thick, almost solid, fog hung a few inches over the ice. Only the American girls were there. In the interest of building up tension, those in charge—i.e., 24/7, i.e., Gil—had decided the ladies shouldn't see each other's routines before the competition.

Gary Gold stood at the barrier, wearing his focused-coach face. At no point did his eyes ever leave Lian. She was currently his top student, a seventeen-year-old Asian-American jumping bean who looked eleven tops and plotted her career with the savvy of a forty-year-old corporate raider. Adopted as an infant from China, Lian was her mother Amanda's only child and, as far as Bex could tell, her only interest in life. Wherever Lian went, her mother was sure to follow. Amanda Reilly was in the stands for every practice, every competition, every exhibition, show, and television interview. When Lian got off the ice, Amanda was by her side, helping Lian dry off her skates, smoothing out the felt rag afterwards and tucking it neatly into Lian's skate bag. She spent a minimum twenty minutes after each session in deep conference with Gary Gold. Bex heard rumors she would even call him at home in the middle of the night if struck by a sudden thought about Lian's training or inspiration for a costume ("What do you think, Gary? Flowers to suggest Lian's blooming as a skater, or butterflies to emphasize her lightness on the ice?").

To be fair, though, this was not a solely Mom-driven enterprise. Lian Reilly herself was famous for expounding to reporters how she had a "master plan" for her career, which included winning the Juvenile Girls Nationals (check), then skipping the intermediate level ("I don't really need it," she patiently explained to Bex during a pre-interview, "It's a superfluous level. As long as you have one title at the junior Nationals level, there's no reason to hang around. You might as well head straight to the big Nationals and start making your name there.") to compete in novice. She placed third in the U.S., her first year there, stayed for a second year in order to win the title, then moved to junior, winning the silver medal before making her senior ladies' debut. Lian's first year in senior, she placed dead last. "That was fine, that was okay," she insisted while the back of her green velvet costume still dripped melting ice chips. "Everyone has to wipe out at one competition to get that psychological block out of the way. I'm happy I've put my wipeout behind me. Now I can focus on never doing that again."

Bex didn't doubt her. Considering the ferociousness with which Lian made all of her pronouncements—she would furrow her brows, thrust out her lower lip and narrow her eyes until her face formed a perfect point, like a Muppet— Bex strongly advised no one to ever doubt her. If Lian said she was going to be the next Senior Ladies Champion of the United States, Bex would happily believe her. Except for one teeny, tiny obstacle.

Named Jordan Ares.

Lian Reilly had never beaten Jordan Ares in any national, international, local, or made-for-television competition. And from the looks of it, that record wasn't about to change. Even here in Moscow, while Lian spent her time on the practice ice doggedly practicing a triple-Toe-Loop/triple-Toe-Loop jump combination over and over again, landing maybe two out of every ten she tried, Jordan, skating a few feet away from her, was landing the much more difficult triple-

Lutz/triple-Toe (the same jump Lian always claimed she'd be doing in her short program, yet never did) with twice the hang time and seemingly half the effort. Everything Jordan did seemed effortless. She didn't so much skate as simply breathe normally while her body floated across the ice of its own volition. She was only four inches taller than the not-quite five-feet-high Lian, but her elegant arms and legs created the illusion that each limb was as long as her competition's entire body. When Lian jumped, she resembled a top spinning in place. When Jordan did, she was like a shooting star. That landed on one foot.

Add to all that Jordan's innate sense of musicality, her all-American blond hair, blue-eyes, pert nose, small chin, and dimples, and the reality that she never got nervous, or even mildly concerned, in competition; and if Jordan said she was going to be the next Senior Ladies Champion of the United States, Bex would also happily believe her. Except for one teeny, tiny obstacle. Also named Jordan Ares.

Because for all of Jordan's talent, very few people in skating could stand her.

And not only for the usual reasons: jealousy, competition, pettiness, resentment, greed, and spite. Those would have been normal and expected. When it came to Jordan, those old favorites were only the tip of the iceberg. In addition to everyone she had ever beaten or had the possibility of beating, Jordan was hated by the USFSA because of her tendency to answer press conference questions in the following manner:

"Jordan, what were you thinking when you fell on that triple Salchow?"

"*F@#&ing ow!*"

She was hated by other parents at the rink because Jordan had declared herself an emancipated minor at the ripe old age of fourteen. The fact that no one had ever set eyes on Mom or Dad, and yet Jordan seemed to be thriving and succeeding nonetheless, was a direct slap in the face of all those who believed it was imperative they be at the rink every single day to monitor and wholeheartedly contribute to their little darling's progress.

But most of all, Jordan was viscerally disliked by every coach in the Professional Skaters Association (PSA). Because, in her eleven-year career, she had been coached by every coach in the PSA. None of those relationships ended happily. Some years, Jordan came to Nationals with one coach, only to leave dramatically with another, and show up with yet a third for Worlds. The fact that she and Igor Marchenko had worked together for almost two years now was actually a story in and of itself. Except now he was dead—so there went that record.

Being newly coach-less, however, did not seem to be holding Jordan back in the slightest as she whipped around the arena. Even after practice was officially over, Jordan continued working on her combination spin, going from Sit to Camel to Scratch and then repeating the entire sequence for extra show-off points. It was only when Gary Gold, upon being assaulted with a dozen questions the minute he stepped away from the barrier, answered a reporter's query about Jordan's future by asserting, "For this competition, I will take over coaching the entire American team; it is the only sensible thing to do," that Jordan skid to a stop and, from across the ice, howled, "The hell you will!"

Within seconds, she was at the barrier, leaning to grab Gary's sleeve with one hand and the reporter's coat with the other. The force of her lunge practically pulled Jordan heels above head over the barrier, but she held on stubbornly with all her might.

Mrs. Reilly frowned distastefully. Not so much at Jordan's actions, as at the fact that Lian hadn't thought of it first. The second Jordan screamed and leapt, every camera at the arena dutifully snapped her picture. Several times. Lian, getting off the ice at the same moment, ended up being a flashbulb-less orphan.

"Did I ask you to coach me, Gold?" Jordan demanded. "I don't remember asking you to coach me."

To his credit, Gary Gold did not, at any point, descend to Jordan's level. Frankly, Bex doubted Gary Gold knew where Jordan's level was. If Ms. Ares was skating's wild-child, then Lian Reilly's coach was its reigning gentleman. Gary Gold never appeared in public—be it at competition, practice session, or picking up the morning paper outside of his door—in anything but the most immaculately pressed suit and tie. His graying hair was always combed, his mustache neatly trimmed. He pronounced every letter in every word—unless the letter was a foreign, silent one, and then he always knew when that was the case (he was the only person Bex ever met who correctly pronounced "forte" as "fort" instead of "fortay"). He did not use contractions. And he certainly never swore.

When Jordan did both in one sentence, then grabbed him for good measure, Gary did not miss a beat. He simply turned around slowly, as if Jordan had politely called his name and inquired, "Did you have something you wished to say to me, Ms. Ares?"

"You're not coaching me, pal." Jordan refused to back down. Though, in the face of Gary's unshakable aplomb, she did somewhat awkwardly let go off his sleeve, resting her hands on the barrier. "All you coach-types do is yell for me to not drop my shoulders or to bend my knees, and then charge mucho bucks for the treat. Hell, I can do that myself and for free."

"You are here, Ms. Ares, as a representative of the United States. And, as long as you are a representative of the United States, you will behave in a certain manner—"

"La-dee-dah."

"If you wish then, yes, la-dee-dah, it shall be."

"I don't have to listen to you. And I can do whatever I want, you can't stop me," Jordan stressed dramatically, and attempted to stomp off. Bex used the word attempted because no matter how emphatic her parting words and how theatrical the toss of her head, it was still almost impossible to truly, effectively stomp off while wearing skating boots and trying to pull off said stomp while teetering atop bright orange blade-guards.

A few of the reporters attempted to pursue Jordan for a follow-up question. They received a cornucopia of expletives they'd only have to delete and bleep for their trouble. The group that chose to stay rink-side and continue questioning Gary, Bex included, were rewarded by Lian, also awkward atop skate-guards, stepping up to her coach and grinning into the camera lights before remembering that this was a somber occasion and opting for a respectful, concerned look. She waited until all eyes were unquestionably on her before primly telling the press, "You'll have to forgive Jordan. I think she's very upset over Mr. Marchenko's death. She just needs some time to pull herself together."

Mrs. Reilly beamed.

Bex couldn't be sure, but she thought she spied Gary coming as close as he could to rolling his eyes.

Lian waited expectantly for more questions to which she could provide thoughtful yet accessible answers. She grinned into the crowd, eyes darting from right to left, then quickly back to the right, in case she'd missed someone. Once. Twice. There seemed to be no takers. And yet the crowd showed no indication of dispersing, either. Lian looked at them. They looked at Lian. No one said a word.

Bex couldn't take it anymore. She'd always been very bad with uncomfortable silences. She blurted out, "Lian, how do you think Igor Marchenko's death will effect your performance at this competition?"

"Well . . ." Lian's pigtailed head bobbed up and down, condescendingly offering Bex her approval at having asked such an intriguing and perceptive question. "While I think Mr. Marchenko's death was an awful, awful tragedy, and my prayers go out to his friends, family, and countrymen, I don't think it should have much effect on my skating here. I've trained very hard for this competition, and I feel very prepared to go out there, do my best, and have fun!"

Lian looked at Bex, expecting a follow-up or, at the very least, a smile to tell her how well she'd done. Bex couldn't quite go that far with the charade. The best she could manage to muster up by way of a reaction was to glance down at her binder, pretending to be jotting down notes with a gloved hand that didn't even have a pen in it.

Bex putting Lian out of her misery with a token question did the trick in giving the other reporters permission to disperse. As they mumbled in various tongues a phrase that, loosely translated, proved to be, "Who knew it was so cold in an ice rink? Are these people out of their minds spending so much time here?" Bex also attempted to sneak out. Unfortunately for her, Amanda Reilly had other plans.

Though Bex tried to hide behind Sasha, Mrs. Reilly could not be stopped or even slowed down. "Yoo-hoo! Bex! Bex!" she yelled over the heads of the other reporters. Several of them turned around, saw Amanda coming, and proceeded to power-walk like the idiots who every year attempted to outrun the bulls at Pamplona. Bex would have done the same, except that, unlike the temporary figure-skating-enthusiasts here for the gory murder details, she actually had to keep seeing Mrs. Reilly for several more months, if not years. Who knew, some day soon Bex may be asking a favor of Amanda—like a last-minute interview with Lian—and she did not need her mother holding a grudge.

So as the rest of the press corps stampeded past her, Bex forced herself to stop, turn around, and greet Mrs. Reilly with a bright hello. She even introduced her to Sasha, hoping the presence of a total stranger would keep Amanda from launching into whatever issue it was she had with Bex and 24/7 this week.

Amanda nodded politely in Sasha's direction, and mumbled something about his lovely country, how nice it was of

Russia to host them—Lian always enjoyed performing here and she was also a big fan of Russian salad dressing. Then she turned to Bex and, without any sort of preamble, stated, "I certainly hope this Igor fiasco isn't going to affect 24/7's broadcast."

"We have to mention it, Mrs. Reilly."

"Yes. Yes, of course, you have to mention it. I suppose it is news of one sort or another. But 24/7 had better not use that poor man's death as an excuse to simply shove more of that trashy Jordan Ares down the viewing public's throat. I won't stand for it, Bex, I simply won't stand for it!"

"Mrs. Reilly, Jordan is the ranking U.S. and World skater in this competition. The viewing public expects to see—"

"And whose fault is that?"

"Whose fault is what?"

"Don't think I haven't noticed how biased your coverage has always been. From the beginning, 24/7 has been pro-Jordan and anti–my Lian. Don't think we haven't seen it. Last year at Nationals, for instance. Francis and Diana Howarth interviewed Jordan for two minutes and eleven seconds at the conclusion of the competition. They spoke to Lian for only fifty-two seconds."

"Well, Jordan was the silver medallist. Lian was the bronze."

"My poor little girl came back to her hotel room and how long do you think she sobbed over 24/7's slight? How long?"

Bex was very, very tempted to guess, "Uhm . . . twenty-three minutes and sixteen seconds?" But she suppressed the urge. It would set a bad example for Sasha. Instead, she offered, "It wasn't our intention to upset Lian. But protocol—"

"Oh, don't you lie to me, Bex. I know what this is about. And it certainly isn't about any so-called protocol."

"You know what this about," Bex repeated, hoping that

having the words come out of her own mouth might help her make sense of Mrs. Reilly's statement.

Nope. Didn't help at all.

"This is about racism, pure and simple!"

"Racism," Bex echoed. She no longer even phrased it as a question. Bex hoped her dumbfounded expression would silently get the point across.

"The only reason Jordan receives all the press attention is because she is blond and blue-eyed, just like America likes their ladies' champions. It doesn't matter that she can barely skate. It doesn't matter that my Lian has twice the personality and three times the natural talent, not to mention delicate beauty; Jordan gets all the coverage and all the endorsements and all the magazine covers because she's white— white trash, anyone can see that, but still white, I suppose—and my Lian is a proud Asian-American."

"Mrs. Reilly. For one thing, less than a year ago, we did a whole feature on Lian competing at the four continents event in Harbin, China, and going back to visit the orphanage where she was born."

"Tokenism," Mrs. Reilly confidently replied.

"For another, the reason Jordan seems to get more media attention—"

"Not seems. Does. I've made a chart."

"Is because she has been more successful both nationally and internationally."

"Well, what can you expect? The judging panels at most competitions are made up primarily of Americans, Canadians, and Europeans—especially Eastern Europeans. Of course they are going to favor Jordan. It's to be expected. You know what those people are doing to the poor Chechnyans within their own borders! What kind of chance does Lian have in front of judges like that?"

Bex didn't know which issue to tackle first: the sociopolitical origins of Russia's conflict with its breakaway region or Mrs. Reilly's insinuation that skating judges went straight from the ice rink to the killing fields.

"This is just like what happened with Igor and Gary when they were competing as young men," Mrs. Reilly asserted.

"What?" Bex suspected she'd lost the conversation thread among the Caucasus.

"Judges favoring their own kind. Especially those Eastern European judges. The reason Igor always beat Gary is because he was a Russian, and everyone knows that skating-while-Russian is good for a couple of extra points. Always."

"You mean when Igor was still skating for the Soviet Union?"

"And after, too."

"But that doesn't make any sense. The Soviets were furious at Igor for defecting. Why would they hold him up? Wouldn't they want to bury him?"

"It's because they prefer the Soviet style. All those long-sleeved costumes and the dramatic arm-waving and over-done artistic impression every time you turn around. That's the Russian school—frilly, pretty, ballet silliness. Our American way is clearly superior. Power, big jumps, energy; it's what we do best. The Russians couldn't skate like us if their lives depended on it. Our skating is about individuality and freedom. No Russian can duplicate that. But the judging panel is always dominated by the Eastern Europeans, so what chance do we have? It's the same with my Lian and Jordan. Igor Marchenko taught Jordan to do all that interpretive silliness, so the judges always put her first. My Lian has a triple-triple combination, and that seems to count for nothing!"

Bex wanted to offer that perhaps the triple-triple combination might score a few more actual points if Lian actually ever landed it in competition, rather than just compose diary entries about it on her website. But that might have prolonged her encounter with Mrs. Reilly. And no one really wanted that.

"Don't think I don't know that's another reason why 24/7 is always falling all over itself to give the good press to Jordan. It's not even about the skaters. It's about the coaches: 24/7 prefers Igor over Gary, so my poor Lian has to suffer!"

"Why would we prefer Igor over Gary?"

"Oh, you always have. Since the beginning. Everyone just fell so quickly for that poor little brave defector-boy story. That poor little brave defector-boy cost Gary Gold his career, did you know that? Gary could have been our own U.S. and World Champion—multiple times—if it wasn't for Igor. And now the sins of the coaches are being visited on their skaters! Lian is paying for her coach's story not being as interesting as Jordan's coach's story. I ask you, is that Lian's fault? Is it?"

As a rule, Bex did not designate a larger than necessary portion of her brain to the ranting and raving of Amanda Reilly. Rather, she let the verbalized paranoia and self-importance wash over her like a soft, summer breeze over a sparkling lake—or any other yoga-like vision Bex could summon to keep her blood pressure from popping off the top of her head like a cork.

On the other hand, on this particular occasion, somewhere in the midst of her paean to Lian's superiority, Mrs. Reilly seemed to have dropped crumbs of information about a recently deceased man, and a still living man, who certainly had many good reasons not to like the dead guy very much. And, if there was one thing Bex had learned from the last murder and kidnapping she'd stumbled over, that kind of information was terribly useful to have. Especially if you were looking to compile a suspect list.

To that end, she stopped thinking about breezes and lakes, and asked Mrs. Reilly, "Did Gary really resent Igor for defecting?"

"He was furious. Here he was, some poor teenager from Brooklyn—"

Brooklyn?   Mr.-I-Never-Met-a-Long-Vowel-I-Didn't-

Like was from Brooklyn? New York, Brooklyn? That one?
The revelation might be the most shocking thing Bex was
destined to discover on this trip—even if she did find the
murderer.

"—working two jobs just to pay for his skating, and making incredible progress, when, out of nowhere, this Russian
kid just shows up and becomes everyone's pet. Igor got
scholarships. Igor got donations. Igor got Gary's titles and,
eventually, he even got his job! Most parents approach Igor
about coaching long before they ask Gary. They've got it all
wrong, of course. Gary has always been by far the superior
coach, you merely have to look at Lian to realize that. Why,
we wouldn't have switched even if Igor had promised to pay
us! We're sticking with Gary Gold, all the way. It doesn't
matter who people think the number one coach in America
is. It's all about perception, I suppose. It's all about buying
into the myth. That's why prospective students went to Igor
first. That's why Gary's students have the reputation for
being the ones Igor Marchenko didn't want. Not that it's true
in our case, you understand. We've been with Gary since the
beginning. He's been wonderful for Lian. He teaches a nice,
clean, American style. Because he's a real American. But he
can't help that uninformed people seem to prefer the other
type. He can't help it that less loyal students than us left him
for Igor at first opportunity."

"So Gary had a very good reason to kill Marchenko!"

That's odd, Bex mused. Somehow, the thought currently
bouncing around her skull with the subtlety of a Gil Cahill
binder-drop had managed to escape.

And picked up a Russian accent.

Three

It was Sasha who asked the question. And Amanda Reilly who launched into a spirited defense of the man she expected to guide her daughter to fame and fortune. But it was Bex who instantly began pondering the possibility.

"So you think I am correct about this?" Sasha asked as soon as Mrs. Reilly was out of earshot.

"I think," Bex said slowly, plucking each word one at a time, assembly-line-style, in the hope that inspiration might strike during the lengthy pauses, "You . . . definitely . . . have . . . the . . . potential . . . to . . . not . . . be . . . wrong."

"You are saying yes?"

"I am saying . . . maybe."

"Then why did you not just to say *maybe*?"

"Because. While a mind may indeed be a terrible thing to waste, very often, overeducation ain't too great, either."

Sasha stared at Bex not so much blankly, but with obvious concern for her mental health. In retrospect, she supposed that asking a young Russian man, even one aspiring to mini-media-moguldum, to comprehend a reference to the very American United Negro College Fund campaign launched before either of them was even born, may have been a bit much. Especially for his first day.

Bex said, "We need a comprehensive answer about what exactly happened here the morning Igor died. Come on, you're about to get utilized."

Before she leapt on the "Gary Killed Igor" bandwagon—or any bandwagon, for that matter—Bex felt she needed to hear a version of yesterday's events that didn't come from a Russian police station or consisted, in its entirety, of the scribbled words: "Igor Marchenko killed by poison in gloves by unknown person." (Even Sasha appeared a bit surprised at the brevity when he gamely translated the file for Bex. "This is not, I believe, very helpful to you," Sasha offered. "Thanks," she said.)

Bex decided to question Jordan first, because, as Marchenko's student, she in all likelihood had been in closest contact with him immediately prior to his death. Bex also decided to question Jordan first because she was not feeling up to another session with Amanda and her precious Lian. And also because Jordan was the first person Bex saw when she entered the ladies' changing room.

She left Sasha outside to keep watch for the arena's manager, whom Bex also wanted to talk to before she got down to heavy-duty investigating, and barged right in. She'd discovered last season that a television-sponsored, all-access pass *really* meant all-access. Nudity included.

Not that Jordan Ares could be spooked by being caught topless, wearing only hot pink panties, the words "Open All Night" and an arrow printed on the crotch. She didn't even look up when Bex entered the changing room. She was too preoccupied with rifling through her skating bag and cursing about "stupid, crappy, goddamn tape."

"I think it's over there," Bex offered and indicated the floor, where a plastic gold and black audio cassette lay half-obscured by a skate tossed on top of it.

"Hey, thanks!" Either Jordan's medication finally kicked in, or her bipolarism was more pronounced than previously suspected. In any case, she rewarded Bex with a seemingly sincere smile, picked up the tape, tossed it in her bag, and plopped down on a bench beneath the lockers, grabbing an equally hot pink bra (although Bex wondered if one could really call a bra something that didn't so much hold up a nonexistent bust, as merely cover it underneath the translucent tops Jordan usually wore—off the ice and on) and slipping it on. Her hands were behind her back, snapping the hooks, when she asked, "What's up, Tex-Mex?"

Bex figured that was almost her name, and she should go with it.

She said, "I wanted to talk to you about Igor."

"Still dead." Jordan finished with the bra and reached for an orange turtleneck sweater. Bex would have guessed something that color could never work on a girl as pale as Jordan, but the particular shade actually made her (Amanda-detested) blue eyes practically pop from her face, and emphasized the shine of her (pharmaceutically enhanced) blond hair.

"You sound broken up about it."

"Coaches are for suckers. I didn't get emancipated from my own parents to end up with another, *mucho loco parentis*. And this one I had to pay for the abuse, to boot!"

Bex couldn't be certain, but . . . "Jordan, did you just make a joke in both Spanish and Latin?" Bex was sure she'd misunderstood. Surely Jordan, who'd dropped out of school in the seventh grade, did not just pun "in loco parentis," the Latin expression for "in place of parents" used to describe a school's relationship with its pupils, by merging it with the Spanish "loco" for "crazy."

The teen winked. "Makes you pretty sorry for all those times you underestimated me, huh?"

Bex didn't know how exactly to reply to that. So, when in doubt, she stuck to the script she'd entered with. "Jordan, were you with Igor the morning he died?"

"Think I killed him?" Jordan didn't seem offended, just curious.

"Well, I am trying to figure out who did."

"Just like with that judge at Worlds, last year. Yeah, I saw how you broke that on TV. Pretty clever stuff. Sure was more interesting than the snooze-fest exhibition."

"Uhm . . . thanks."

"So you think I offed my own coach?"

"You've fired enough of them."

"Not really the same. Besides, Igor and me got along okay. He didn't do any of that positive reinforcement bull-shit. Like, if I was having a bad day, none of that, 'Aw, sweetie, honey, precious, it's okay, you'll do better next time. And remember, not being able to land your triple/triple doesn't in any way devalue you as a person. So you run on back to Mommy-kins and tell her who the bestest coach in the world is, and how much he wuv, wuv, wuvs you. Oh, by the way, check's due. Hand it over.' If I was having a bad day with Igor, he told me, 'You're having a crappy day, Jordan, get it together or I'm not coming back tomorrow.'"

"A lot of people wouldn't exactly consider that a positive," Bex pointed out.

"I was paying Igor to coach, not coddle me. I want to win. I know how fantastic a human being I am; I don't need to hire somebody to patronize me. You think I want to end up like Lian? Her mother and Gary spend so much time kissing up and telling her how superduper she is, how's she supposed to get motivated to skate better? Mrs. Reilly thinks the judges prefer me to Lian because I have big eyes and white skin? Try, because I don't cheat my jumps. I work hard to make sure I don't give those judges any excuse to mark

down my technique. Lian, though, she's won so many pid-
dly junior titles with her lousy jumps, she doesn't get why
no one is falling for them in seniors. Her mom won't tell her
because she thinks Lian walks on water—the not frozen
kind, I mean. And Gary won't tell her because Mrs. Reilly
won't let him, and he needs the money."

"Is that why you don't want Gary coaching you here? Because you think he's a bad coach, or because you think he's
under Mrs. Reilly's control?"

"I'm telling you, and I'm telling everyone, I don't need
another coach! I am sick and tired of being told what to do
and what to wear and how to behave. When am I going to be
allowed to make my own choices and have my own opin-
ions? What the hell do you all want from me? Enough is
enough, okay?"

For a minute, Jordan looked to be close to tears. She
blinked. She looked away.

She reached two fingers into her left eye, plucked out a
contact lens, popped it in to her mouth, sucked briefly, then
slid it back onto her pupil. She blinked again. Bex forcibly
swallowed the sympathy that had been threatening to well
up within her chest, not unlike phlegm from a bad cold.

"Okay. So. Anyway, Jordan, the reason I came in was, I
was hoping you could give me some details about what was
going on here the morning Igor died. The police report is
very sketchy. I don't think they actually interviewed anyone
about it."

"I know they didn't talk to me. I don't *govori* the *russki*."

"Well, I'm interviewing you, now, so please, pay attention."

"Yes, ma'am." Jordan offered her version of the straight
leg goose-step still done by the pimpled young soldiers
around Lenin's tomb. While wearing only a sweater and hot
pink panties. It made for an interesting sociopolitical com-
mentary.

"Right. Good. So, let's start at the beginning. Did you

and Igor come over to the arena together from the hotel that morning?"

"What? You think I'm Lian and Gary? Igor and I are not joined at the hip. I can wipe my own butt, and I can find the rink all by my blond little self."

"Good to know." Bex opened her spiral notebook and wondered if she should be writing: Jordan Ares would like it on the record that she can wipe her own butt. "So you and Igor met up at the arena? Who arrived first, you or him?"

Jordan cocked her head to the side, seemingly actually thinking about her answer rather than blurting it out, for a change. "Him. He got here first. Because when I came in, I saw him talking to Mrs. Reilly. Which was pretty weird."

"Igor was talking to Amanda Reilly? Why?"

"I don't know. They both clammed up the moment I walked in."

"Were Gary and Lian around?"

"I don't think so. No. No, they couldn't have been. Because if Lian was already on the ice, no way would Mommy have been looking anywhere else. Lian was probably getting changed here in the locker room or something. Don't know where Gary was."

"And then what did you do?"

"I gave Igor my gloves."

"What? Why?" Considering gloves were at the very center of this extravaganza, Jordan was awfully casual about bringing the topic up.

"Take a chill pill, Bex. I said I gave him *my* gloves. I didn't touch his. I always give them to him at the beginning of a session. He puts them on the radiator for me, next to his. He said his coach used to tell him to do it, to warm them up for after practice, and now he's got me doing it, too."

"So, you knew that Igor's gloves would be on the radiator?"

"Me and the entire world knew. He's only been doing it for a million years."

"Did anyone touch the gloves while they were on the radiator?"

"Well, off the top of my head, I'm going to guess the person who killed him."

"Thank you, Jordan, that's very helpful. What I mean is, did you see anyone who could have put the poison—"

"It wasn't poison," Jordan said. "It was foxglove. It's a homeopathic treatment for people with heart conditions."

"Yes, I know that, I read the police report. . . . How did you know that, Jordan?"

"I can read, too, believe it or not. It was in that free newspaper they give us at the hotel. And it's what everybody's talking about around here, this morning. Except, as usual, the skating simpletons have got it wrong. Foxglove isn't a poison. It's how they make the heart drug digitalis. Igor just got too much of it. Probably a concentrated form, I'd bet. That's what killed him."

"You're doing this bit for my benefit, aren't you?" Bex couldn't imagine another reason. "You're messing with me. You want me to think you killed Igor."

"You think I'm mental?"

"I'm not ready to discount the possibility."

"Well, I definitely am. But not about this. I've got some butts to kick this week, I've got no time for side trips to the police station."

"So when did you become an expert on homeopathic medicine?"

"Duh. See above. Jordan can read. I know what foxglove is. Is that a crime? I can also spell *supercalifragilisticexpialidocious*, and *potato*. I know that the formula for water is H-two-O and the average rainfall of Mongolia. I love knowledge. I yearn for it."

"That's why you dropped out of school?"

"That's exactly why I dropped out of school. If a piece of knowledge accidentally wanders into a classroom it gets stomped down before drawing a breath."

"So what is the average rainfall in Mongolia?"

"Two hundred sixteen millimeters a month."

"Okay. Fine. I'm convinced. You're a self-taught savant. You know a plethora of things, including tons of details about the drug that killed your umpteenth coach, but that's just a coincidence. Yes, Jordan, I believe you, you're not messing with me at all."

"Didn't say I wasn't messing with you." Jordan smiled. No. She grinned. In a rather evil manner.

"Can we get back to the conversation, please?"

"Weren't we talking about what evil villain might have been lurking around the radiator, looking for a chance to slip some funky homeopathy into Igor's gloves?"

"Did you see anyone?"

"Not a soul."

Bex sighed.

Jordan, perhaps sensing that her interrogator's patience was wearing thin and that all this lovely attention was at risk for being withdrawn, deigned to add, "I wasn't really looking, though. I was on the ice. Lian was on the ice. Igor and Gary were standing at the barrier. Mrs. Reilly was wandering around. TV people were running wires and some arena people were doing whatever it is they do to get ready. Everything looked normal."

Bex was afraid of that. Just like a serial killer who stashed seventeen bodies in his basement and made puppy-dog models out of their hair always had neighbors willing to tell the press, "He was so quiet and unassuming, we never dreamed anything odd was going on," in her experience, a murder scene was always equally full of people happy to report, "Everything was normal. Until they found the body."

"Bex!" The voice came from outside the changing room. Sasha was too polite to barge in, though his temporary association with television gave him all rights to. "Please to come out, now! I am holding to the Shura. You wished to speak to him, yes?"

Bex did wish to speak to the arena manager, yes. She bade Jordan a quick good-bye and stepped outside the changing room door. To discover that, as advertised, Sasha was, indeed, "holding to the Shura." Bex's runner had the arena manager by the arm, one hand on his elbow, the other on his shoulder, and had backed him bodily into a corner.

"Shura is here to speak with you." Sasha proudly pushed the sixty-something man forward. Dressed in a thick, brown, down coat buttoned up to above his chin and a black cap pulled down below his brows, Shura appeared to be all scowl, slit eyes, and a bulbous nose decorated with the relief map of every vodka he'd ever guzzled. He didn't so much speak, as gargle, cough, and expectorate. Of course, to be fair, he was gargling, coughing, and expectorating in Russian, so maybe the words were supposed to sound like that.

"Shura says he does not know anything," Sasha translated.

"That's okay," Bex smiled her most multicultural, all-men-are-brothers smile. "I still want to ask him some questions. Maybe he'll remember something important."

Sasha translated her words into Russian. Shura's glare in response suggested he did not believe that would be happening.

"Could you please ask him if he saw—"

Before Bex was finished asking her question, Shura exploded with an answer that, frankly, did not sound precisely on point. He waved his arms. He stomped his feet. He pointed at Bex. He pointed at himself and at several 24/7 crew members milling around, and at the Russian flag hanging above the doorway. And then at the toilet down the hall.

"I see . . ." Bex thought to herself.

"Shura is saying," Sasha attempted to translate while the tirade was still going on, "that he thinks all of Marchenko's murder will be blamed on Russia, because Americans always to blame everything on the Russia. Shura speaks for all the people of Russia and he says Marchenko was . . . what is word, please, for human excrement?"

"Shit!" Shura shouted. Obviously, he knew some English and also knew when to use it for maximum effectiveness. "Shit! Igor Marchenko is shit! He to treats Mother Russia like shit!"

Bex wondered if she should be writing that down. Next to Jordan's informative point about being able to wipe her own ass. Her investigation was definitely developing a theme.

His own scatological point gotten across, Shura returned to shouting in Russian, this time speaking even faster, as if daring Sasha to keep up.

"Shura says Marchenko show no respect for the homeland that trained him to be a great and successful athlete. He defects to America for money only and he forget to who he owed a debt. Marchenko throw the World Champion medal he won for Russia in the toilet. Shura does not think Marchenko treat his American medals with such disrespect."

Shura stopped talking, crossed his previously flailing arms, and looked expectantly at Bex. She, in turn, looked at Sasha, waiting for him to translate the final, summary bit.

"Marchenko is shit," Sasha concluded.

"I see."

"And also Shura says that he sees this: it was Gary Gold who put Marchenko's gloves on the heater, not Marchenko, himself."

"*You* were just waiting to spring that last part on me, weren't you?" Bex teased Sasha as the newly released Shura stomped down the hallway. "You made me listen to all that 'shit,' just so you could deliver the Gary Gold part for maximum drama."

"We Russians. We are dramatic people. Very passionate." Sasha smiled at Bex. And suddenly, he no longer looked fourteen years old. In fact, Bex wasn't sure how she could have ever thought he was anything but . . .

"Sasha," Bex interrupted their regularly scheduled murder-solving to indulge her unexpected curiosity. "How old are you?"

"Twenty-four."

"You're my age?" Bex yelped. Here she'd been treating him like he was some kid sent to do her bidding, and he was actually her own age!

"If you are twenty-four, that is correct."

"I'm sorry. I thought you were—"

"Young. Yes. Everyone to say this. Young face, they say."

"It's just that we usually hire teenagers for these runner jobs, so that's why I—"

"Is fine. I know. Job said student. I to lie to them. Use young face to advantage. They are asking, you attending university? I say yes. Is true. Am attending university. This job will help to pay for university."

"Graduate school?"

"No. I tell them truth, again. I am in first year. When I first leave my orphanage, I work as street cleaner. But I save my money for university. Ten years, I have enough."

Bex was sure she must have misheard. The numbers didn't add up. "You had to save up ten years to go to college? Since you were fourteen?"

"Yes. Fourteen, no more orphanage."

"You're an orphan?"

"I live in orphanage," Sasha repeated. Then he explained, "I am six, mother leave our home. Father not happy, begins drinking. Sometimes, he forgets to come home. The police, they bring me to orphanage. I am not orphan like in the infant fairy stories. My parents are alive. I think. But I to live in orphanage as child. You see?"

Bex saw. Thanks to her own childhood which had been wasted with her nose permanently wedged in the "infant fairy stories," along with Dickens, Brontë, Twain, Rowling (so, fine, so she read a couple of *Harry Potters* when she was already halfway through college—no crime in that), Sasha's mentioning "orphan" instantly flooded Bex's mind's eye with Technicolor images of urchins begging for more gruel, dead best friends, escapes on rafts, and, well . . . wizards. She realized Sasha had probably experienced none of those things—was there a Russian equivalent of gruel, for instance? But, nevertheless, Bex found his background overwhelming. What was the correct response after being told someone was an orphan? "I'm sorry," didn't seem exactly adequate, especially since he'd helpfully pointed out his parents weren't even really dead. What was Bex supposed to say to him now?

"Is Shura certain he saw Gary put Marchenko's gloves on the heater?"

Yes. After much soul-searching, that was the sensitive response Bex had decided to go with. She wasn't proud of it, but there it was.

"That is what he says." Sasha did not even blink at her abrupt change of subject. Bex wondered if her panicked duck-and-cover was typical of people learning the young man in front of them had been abandoned and institutionalized.

"That could be a pretty big clue. If it's true," Bex noted as she was also juggling the knowledge that Sasha wasn't some green college kid who needed to be mentored by her experienced self, but a contemporary who had probably logged more life experience in a year than Bex had to date. So who exactly was supposed to be teaching whom, here? After all, they were in Sasha's home country, dealing with the murder of his fellow countryman, and interrogating witnesses in a language Bex didn't even know. Maybe she should step back and let him lead for a while?

Nope. Bex gave the notion a split second's thought. Nope, couldn't do that.

She told Sasha, "We need to search Igor's room. He

might have something in there that could help us figure out who wanted him dead."

"Very well," Sasha replied, as unfazed as ever. Sasha, Bex was beginning to realize, was a very go-with-the-flow kind of guy. And, since that was the case . . .

"Any idea how we can get in? I mean, I don't have a key or anything."

"Is not a problem," Sasha said. "You are in Russia."

Sasha was right. All they needed to gain access to Igor Marchenko's room was for Sasha to exchange a few words with the floor matron who sat at a desk at the end of the hall, watching the guests coming and going and glaring at them disapprovingly—just in case. Well, that and for Bex to exchange a few hundred rubles with the lovely lady, as well. As they walked down the hall, key in hand, Bex made a note in her reimbursement book, even as she wondered how she would phrase what she'd used the money for. Bribe did seem to be such an ugly word. Maybe she should call it . . . a tip?

Sasha opened Marchenko's door, held it gallantly open for Bex to pass through, then whistled loudly and, with a grin, tossed their illicit key back to the floor matron, who managed to catch the sliver of metal without breaking her glare. Sasha continued smiling at her. Until finally, reluctantly, she smiled back. Sasha winked and blew her a kiss. The sour-faced woman smiled for real. Bex didn't know what to make of the exchange. All she knew was, she kind of liked it.

"Where do we to start?" Sasha asked.

"Well . . ." Bex looked around the room, furnished in generic hotel: double bed, end table, chair, threadbare bits of string sticking up from the green rug. And the bedspread. And the curtains. And the molding in the corners. It felt like the whole place needed to be mowed, or at least shaved.

Igor's things were still where he had apparently dumped

them before heading out to the arena the day before. Obviously, the local *militsia* did not expect to find any clues here. One suit was hanging in the closet. The rest of his things spilled out of the suitcase he'd loaded atop the rusted luggage stand. Bex spied several undershirts, three pairs of black socks tied into balls, some folded boxer shorts. That seemed indecent, somehow. Here the man was dead, and Bex was standing around, gawking at his underwear. Even worse, she was trying to get psyched enough to actually roll up her sleeves and rifle though his underwear. Though she wasn't sure what exactly she expected to find in there.

Sasha said, "Here are his personal things. This may to help, yes?"

Bex had been so busy pondering the philosophical implications of a dead man's boxers, she'd managed to miss that lying propped up against the suitcase was a smaller, leather bound case, the size of a legal-sized envelope, but thicker. It seemed to contain several small jewelry-sized boxes, as well as a thick wad of papers. In Bex's extensive, crime-solving experience, a thick wad of papers beat underwear and socks for relevancy any day of the week.

She grabbed the case and plopped down on the bed. Sasha plopped down next to her, looking over Bex's shoulder, his chin brushing her sweater, the slight stubble there raking it audibly. A few hours earlier, when she had thought he was younger than her, he'd sat this close to her in the cab, and Bex had barely noticed he was there—he might have been just another piece of the shabby black leather they were both trying not to stick to. Now that she knew he was actually her own age and not the naïve kid she'd been comfortable with, the proximity suddenly seemed too . . . proximal.

"Ahem," Bex said. She shrugged to get away from him, hopefully without it looking like she was shrugging to get away from him, and dove into the case. She pulled out a stack of papers, some stapled, some paper-clipped, and attempted to sort them by category. She found several billing

slips for lessons, along with receipts and his rink's private
ice schedule for the next month. Bex put those items behind
her. When she did so, her hand accidentally brushed Sasha's,
who was reaching for them at the same time as Bex was dis-
carding them. Bex withdrew her hand quickly. Hopefully
without, you know, looking like she was withdrawing it
quickly.

The next group of documents was all photocopies. There
were several copies of Igor's American passport, his natu-
ralization papers, his U.S. tax records, the lease to his Connecticut condominium, an electric bill, plus a notarized
letter from his congressman, testifying to Igor Marchenko's
good citizenship and legal residency. The man may have
smiled for the cameras that greeted him at the Moscow airport, but he was obviously not as confident about being allowed to leave as he appeared. The Union of Soviet Socialist
Republics may have been almost fifteen years gone, but Igor
Marchenko wasn't willing to bet his life that they'd given up
all of their strong-arm tactics. If the Russians tried to keep
him by force, Igor was obviously ready to fight back with a
mountain of American paperwork. Bex was surprised he
hadn't toted along a red, white, and blue flag to wave.

Oh. Wait. She spoke too soon. There it was.

She opened one of the ring-sized, velvet jewelry boxes to
find a pair of American flag cufflinks. A second box re-
vealed a "USA" tie clip. A third held the 2005 skating
team's official pin (featuring a flag—natch—wrapped
around a skate), and the fourth a 1977 U.S. World Figure
Skating Team pin.

"Nineteen-seventy-seven." Bex double-checked his paperwork to make sure. "That was the year he defected. This
must be from his first World Team." She picked up the shiny
2005 pin, comparing it to the well-worn, 28-year-old one.
"His first team, and his last one. That's pretty sad."

But Sasha didn't seem to be listening to her wax philosophical. While she'd been pondering the finite nature of

man, he'd reached into the bottom of Igor's case and pulled out what, from the back, appeared to be a cashier's check. Naturally, when he did so, his proximity to her shoulder and/or hand decreased. Which was good. Right?

Sasha stared quizzically at the rectangular strip of paper in his hand. Slowly, he said, "Igor Marchenko, he is the coach of Jordan, yes?"

"Yes."

"And Amanda Reilly, she is the mother of Lian?"

Bex's heart began to beat faster as she temporarily (really, it was only temporary) forgot her manners and grabbed the cashier's check out of Sasha's hand. She scanned the signature line. And finished Sasha's thought for him. "Why then, is Igor Marchenko in possession of a check made out in his name and signed by Lian Reilly's mother?"

Four

"Do you know what this means?" Bex asked excitedly.

"No!" Sasha said, with equal enthusiasm.

"Me, neither!" She took a deep breath, crossed her legs, Indian-style, to fit more comfortably on the bed, and calmed down. "But, it's got to mean something, right?"

"Of course, yes."

Bex cocked her head to one side and considered his cheerful, enthusiastic visage. "You're just patronizing me, aren't you?"

"Of course, yes." Sasha agreed. Still cheerful. Still enthusiastic. Still smiling. Bex wondered if she was being deliberately charmed as effectively as the elderly floor-matron of a few moments earlier. Back then, Sasha's purpose had been to secure their entry to Marchenko's room. But what could his current purpose be? Because, certainly, there had to be a purpose. People just didn't go around charming Bex for no reason.

"I think we need to speak to Amanda Reilly," Bex decided. She realized she had just triumphantly declared the obvious. But it still felt good to have a plan.

"Let us go and find her!" Sasha matched Bex tone for tone. He bounced off the bed and offered her his elbow, as if heading towards a formal dinner.

Bex took it. Feeling silly. And kind of charmed.

Drat.

Amanda Reilly, however, was nowhere to be found. Bex and Sasha checked the arena. They checked the hotel. Finally, Bex had a brainstorm and checked with a harried 24/7 production assistant in the makeshift 24/7 production office.

Rather than shipping a fully equipped, American satellite truck to Russia and incurring the gigantic expense of such an endeavor, 24/7 had taken a risk and rented a local news truck, hoping it could get the job done for less cost. After less than thirty seconds inside said truck, they all quickly realized that it could not get the job done. And not just because the interior reeked of vodka, borsht, and a culture that did not believe in deodorant. That, they presumably could have all gotten used to. The larger problem was that, in this particular production trailer, there were no chairs. Not by the monitors. Not by the desks. Not in the editing bay. They could tell there had once been chairs. The ragged maws from where they'd been ripped out were still visible (and sharp—how come their Russian/English dictionaries didn't include, "Please, may I have a tetanus shot?").

"Where are the chairs?" Gil had asked the local man who'd provided them with these top-of-the-line vehicles.

"We do not sit, in Russia," the local man helpfully explained with an absolutely straight face. While sitting.

Well, unfortunately, in the United States of America, sitting was, like, one of their favorite things. Even the penny-pinching Gil had to agree with that. So the satellite truck was scrapped in favor of squatting inside the arena's underground offices. Unfortunately, instead of the long, narrow space offered by a good production trailer, they were stuck with a half dozen tiny, windowless rooms. That also smelled of vodka and borsht. Gil took the largest cell, and the rest were assigned by seniority. Bex got nothing, because, according to Gil, "You should be out in the arena, getting us information. Besides, I just heard somewhere that they don't sit in Russia. You don't want to offend anyone."

The production assistants got no offices, either. Their job was to scamper from one room to another, fetching the (self-) important producers whatever they wanted, preferably before they even knew they wanted it. At 24/7, if a production assistant was not moving, he was presumed to be goofing off. Which was why getting one to stop and respond to a question was notoriously difficult. Like in a 1980s Atari game with a frog trying to cross the road, Bex had to literally lurk at the edge of the dim hallway, watching the P.A.s zooming by in every direction, before spotting one she believed small enough and slow enough that Bex decided yeah, she could take her. She jumped out into traffic to block the girl's path with her body.

After the perfunctory shriek, the P.A., who was juggling a milk crate full of Beta tapes, confirmed Bex's hunch that Lian and her mother were out wandering the streets of Moscow while a 24/7 camera crew and producer lapped up every touristy moment.

"Where did they go?" Bex asked.

"I'm not sure." The girl lost her grip on the milk crate, sending tapes sprawling to the ground. Bex crouched down to help her clean. And to continue her interrogation. The P.A. recalled, "We wanted to shoot the usual. You know, Saint Basil's, Red Square, Lenin's Tomb, Russia One-O-One. Stuff that when people look at it, they go, oh, yeah, that's Moscow. But Mrs. Reilly was concerned that, because Lian was Chinese, if they posed in Red Square, it would suggest a tacit endorsement of Communism in China." The P.A. stopped what she was doing, looking at Bex as if she'd just heard her own words for the first time. "That's nuts. I mean, isn't it?"

Bex knew how she felt. Spending any amount of time around either skating or television people also made her doubt her own judgment. When everyone around you thought the insane was reasonable, it tended to play funny tricks with your mind.

"It is nuts," Bex reassured. She picked up two Beta tapes and tossed them into the milk crate. She noticed that one tape had a yellow sticker on the side with the red magic-marker scrawl, "Marchenko—Early Worlds Footage."

Bex asked, "Gil is still planning on doing the Marchenko piece?"

"Oh, yeah. He thinks the murder will make a great button."

A button on a feature was considered the perfect ending to the story—one line or image to summarize everything that had gone before. How nice of Igor Marchenko—or, actually, his killer—to provide Gil with a moment of video nirvana.

"We're going to start cutting Marchenko's piece today. I guess, if we had to, we could leave it unfinished till the weekend show. But, honestly, Bex, see, it would make it a lot easier for me if you could have the murderer figured out by maybe tomorrow—tops? I'm really swamped here, and if I knew which exact footage I needed in advance, like, if we had the killer already on tape, it would make my life a lot easier."

Bex looked at her for a good, long while. She considered many different answers. None of them seemed quite right. She finally said, "I'll see what I can do."

"Great."

"Yeah. Listen," Bex straightened up. "Do you have any idea when Amanda and Lian are scheduled to be back?"

"I guess as soon as they find a spot that doesn't make Amanda think it looks like Lian condones Communism. That's also, you know, pretty."

Oh, wonderful. That could be any time between now and . . . much later than now. In case it wasn't obvious, Bex was not a big fan of spinning her wheels. When she got it into her mind that something needed to be done, she insisted it needed to be done—with all due respect to Gil Cahill's pet phrase—"now, now, now!" Granted, that was primarily because, if Bex did not do something right away, she was likely to forget about it as soon as the next "now, now, now!" situation reared its head. But the point still remained. Bex had decreed she needed to speak to Amanda Reilly. Therefore Amanda Reilly should be available to her immediately.

"And where do you think that might be?" Bex pressed, as if upping the insistency of her tone might wring the P.A. into producing an answer she had no way of knowing.

"I have no way of knowing that," the P.A. confirmed.

Up until that point, Sasha had been standing by unobtrusively. He was very good at that. He didn't so much blend into the proverbial woodwork, as into thin air. He was there. Of course, he was there; anybody could see that. And yet, like the waiter in a fancy restaurant or the grocery-store clerk ringing up orange juice and bananas before whom most people continued having extremely personal conversations that they'd never dream of revealing in front of anyone else, Sasha possessed that aura of appearing so involved in something else, that he wouldn't dream of eavesdropping on you. That is until, out of the blue, he piped up and demonstrated how that wasn't the case at all.

"Excuse me." Sasha cleared his throat and aimed that dazzling smile of his at the P.A. Coincidentally, Bex found herself thinking, *You know, I've never really liked this P.A. Even though this is our first complete conversation ever.* He continued, "Excuse me, but I am Moscow native. Perhaps, if you would to give myself a mobile telephone number of the cameraperson who is with Mrs. Reilly, I can to call them and make suggestions for pretty places where they may shoot. That are not Communist."

Bex wanted to kiss him.

Because of his cleverness in coming up with a plan that would put them in contact with Lian Reilly, of course.

"Sounds cool. I'll get you the number," the P.A. said.

When she turned around to grab the cell phone contact sheet off Gil's desk, Bex pivoted to face Sasha, grinning madly and mentally jumping up and down. He winked at her in return.

"We are good team?" he whispered.

"We are good team," Bex swore.

"Here you go." The P.A. used the tip of her nail to indicate a multi-digit number four lines from the bottom. She turned to Sasha, "Thanks for your help, man."

"It is no problem." He half-bowed gallantly, and smiled as she walked away.

Yup. It was official. Bex really did not like that P.A.

She pulled out her cell phone and promptly dialed the necessary numbers. Only to receive an automated message informing her that the party she was seeking was out of zone. Well, how the heck was that helpful?

"My idea, not so good?" Sasha asked.

"Your idea good," Bex reassured. "Your country's phone system, not so great."

"I am sorry."

"It's okay. I guess I'll just have to bite the bullet and wait for them to come back. I've got other stuff to do, anyway, I guess. The two Russian girls are practicing at the arena right now. I suppose I should head over there and confirm their program elements, so we don't have an announcing fiasco during the live broadcast."

"Because the announcers who talk, they do not lift their heads from the binders?"

"I love a man who listens to my ranting," Bex said.

And then she said nothing at all. Because she couldn't think of anything to follow up her declaration with.

Sasha, on the other hand, did not seem at all rattled by her declaration of devotion—facetious though it may have been. He simply nodded his head and asked, "Will you be to needing me for this?"

Bex couldn't think of any reason why she should.

So, naturally, she said, "Oh, most definitely."

They arrived at the arena as the Russian competitors, dressed in matching team jackets of red, white, and blue (though with far different implications than all the theme paraphernalia in Marchenko's room), were stretching rinkside, bobbing up and down as they jogged in place and lacing up their custom-made boots in anticipation of taking the ice. Just like in the U.S., where Jordan and Lian were battling to stake their claim on the newly vacant Nationals title after the retirement of World Silver Medalist Erin Simpson, in Russia the concurrent retirement of long-(long!)-time European champion Xenia Trubin had also opened the field to a successor. The two favorites had been invited to take on Jordan and Lian in this no-points, no-stakes, braggingrights-though-just-barely, made-for-TV competition. Judging from the determined looks on their faces, however, both girls were taking the event as seriously as the final group at the World Championship.

Contestant number one, Galina Semenova, was fourteen years old, the reigning Junior World Champion. A four-foottall redhead with the build of a leprechaun and the face of a chubby-cheeked stacking doll, she could also jump like a top NBA dunker and twirl like a human dreidel. She'd landed a quadruple Toe-Loop to win her Junior World title—and celebrated by spontaneously having her skates dyed gleaming gold—and had been practicing quadruple Salchows in the warm-up of every competition she'd entered.

Not that she actually intended to attempt one in her Long
program. It was too risky at this point and probably wouldn't
even be adequately rewarded. But it helped rattle the other
girls on the ice, and that, more often than not, was a good
enough consequence. It was an indisputable fact that young,
freckle-faced Galina could jump. What was also an indisputable fact was that she couldn't actually skate worth a
damn.

Galina Semenova did not glide, she trudged. Her tracings
on the ice were not the graceful lobes and figures from
which the sport once got its name, but straight, flat lines, as
if made by a Communist-era people's tractor. When obligated, in the course of a well-balanced program, to execute
an element that wasn't a jump—say, a spin, or a spiral, or a
footwork sequence—Galina's rosy-cheeked, elfin face
would narrow until her eyebrows were practically kissing.
And then she would bulldoze her way thought the mandatory unpleasantness. The quicker to get back to the jumping.

Galina's main competition, on the other hand, was a
skater who, prior to taking off into the air, actually appeared
to sigh with resignation, visibly distressed that someone had
insisted on forcing athleticism into what should have been
an exclusively lyrical art form. Her style was more balletic,
more peaceful, more classically Russian. Which is what
made it extra special amusing that this upholder of Russia's
centuries-old traditions bore the oh-so-Russian name of
Brittany Monroe.

Seventeen-year-old Brittany had, up until two years earlier, skated for the United States. This made sense, seeing as
how she'd been born and raised in Cleveland, Ohio. But, unfortunately, her aversion to jumping didn't win her any
friends in the American judging circles. She constantly finished out of the top five at the U.S. Nationals, which made
her chances of qualifying for the World Team practically nil.
So young Brittany did what any elite athlete would when
faced with the prospect of not achieving her goals in a

timely manner: she cheated. Well, technically, it wasn't really cheating. Brittany simply rummaged around in her family tree and dredged up a maternal grandfather who had been born in Russia before emigrating at the ripe old age of two and a half. She then declared it her lifelong dream to "regain" her Russian citizenship. Once that was done, Brittany entered Russian Nationals where, thanks to the fact that the best female skaters in Russia were traditionally sent to do Pairs or Dance, she was able to make the top three and earn a spot on their World Team. And to think, all Brittany had to do to achieve her goals was give up her American citizenship. Bex idly wondered what Igor Marchenko, who'd endured so much to achieve the opposite, had thought about her flip-flop.

Sasha said, "What would you like me to do here?"

Just for fun, they'd entered the arena from the top instead of the bottom this time around. Rather than coming up through the gray tunnels, with their endless, gray rooms decorated with chewed up, green carpeting, stripped bare light bulbs, and furniture that looked as if a hoard of midgets came every night to kick it, they'd walked in above the top row of seats, so that the entire arena lay open at their feet. The view was definitely much less depressing. Seen from above, the dents in the metal chairs didn't seem quite as gloomy. You might even pretend there was a modern art pattern involved. And the ice surface itself was more visibly of Olympic quality, a white oval so gleaming and smooth it was practically blinding. Though you could still see where the barrier around it had formerly been inscribed with the Cyrillic, inspirational words, "Long Live Our Glorious Communist Party of the Union of Soviet Socialist Republics." Now, it was three-quarters covered with ads for McDonald's, Kit Kat, and Coca-Cola.

Sasha asked, "Please say where you would like me to go."

Bex considered her options. In theory, all she really

needed to do was check with the girls or their coaches that she had all of their elements correct and in the proper order. Of course, considering how often some skaters gave her what she could only guess were the elements to somebody else's program, it also helped if she stayed around long enough to watch them do a run-through and confirm. But, in practical terms, being at the arena during the Russian session was also a prime opportunity for Bex to follow up on Shura's profanity-laced rant and investigate whether all of Igor Marchenko's ex-countrymen felt so vitriolic about the late coach—and how they might have expressed those emotions.

Looking a few rows above the ice, Bex spotted Valeri Konstantin, the president of the Russian Figure Skating Federation. The man who she, in her more whimsical moments, liked to think of as Ferret Head. (Was it her fault that his comb-over looked like a rodent toupee? Bex thought not.)

Bex made an on-the-spot decision. She told Sasha, "Look, do me a favor. Would you take this list of elements down to the girls' coaches and confirm that I've got them all correct? I need to talk to someone for a minute."

"Do you need my translation help?"

"No, it's alright. He speaks okay English. I've interviewed him before. Besides, I think he might be more open with me if I'm alone. The questions I'm planning to ask, I don't think he'll want an audience for."

"Understood," Sasha said. He accepted Bex's binder from her, tucked it under his arm along with the pen she offered, and proceeded to march straight down to the ice to do as she'd asked. Yup, Bex really, really liked that boy.

Making sure that there was no one around who might overhear them, Bex casually yet purposefully made her way over to Valeri Konstantin. He saw her coming, but made no attempt to duck. To be honest, he appeared to be in no mood to do much of anything. The president of the most influential figure skating federation on the planet looked very tired. And not more than a little bored.

He was a rotund man, with jowls that wobbled around his neck like laundry on the line, and a square, sopping sponge of a body that was painfully squeezed into the arena's thinly padded chairs. As she studied the situation, Bex wondered how Konstantin intended to ease back out again. In addition, the weight of his ferret-like comb-over also seemed to be compressing his head deep into his neck, so that the jowls of his chin were brushing the tips of his shoulders as he gallantly fought to keep his eyes open and trained on his two best hopes for a Russian-dominated ladies' skating future.

"Hello, Mr. Konstantin," Bex offered brightly as she plopped down next to him.

"Ha," he replied.

"I'm Bex Levy. The 24/7 researcher? We've met before. I interviewed you last month for our feature on the evolution of Russia's skating program?"

"Ga," he conceded.

Bex had been meaning to politely inquire if it would be okay for her to ask him a few questions. But considering her record so far, she decided to dive right in and see if she could coax out more than random syllables.

Bex said, "Your girls are looking strong this year. Galina Semenova is so young and already she's got such potential!"

"Hmph," Konstantin said. Bex was about to try another approach when, as if he'd been slapped on the back to keep from choking, he spat out, "This girl is the best jumper in the world. Fourteen years old, and already the best in the world. Quads, here, quads, there—"

Bex wondered if there was an American alive who would have blamed her for nodding her head and solemnly observing, "Everywhere a quad-quad." Still, she decided to suppress the impulse.

"But it is the judging system that does not esteem such excellent athleticism," Konstantin continued. "It is not logi-

cal to give as many points for the good doing of a spin,
which is much easier skill to perfect than the good doing of
quadruple jump."

Bex asked, "A year ago, when Xenia Trubin was still
competing, didn't you tell the press that it was unfair to
judge an entire skating program on how many jumps a girl
did, because there was more to a balanced routine than just
jumps?"

"Sha," Konstantin said.

Well. That certainly went swimmingly.

At least Bex now knew that they had no discernible rap-
port to disturb if she went ahead and actually asked him the
hard questions.

"Igor Marchenko's invitation to come to Moscow for this
event was issued by the Russian Skating Federation." Bex
asked, "Does that mean it came from you?"

Konstantin shrugged and said, "Ares will not come without her coach, Marchenko. We need Ares here. She is
number three in the world. Number one after Trubin and
Simpson retired last year. Semenova must compete against
the best, for us to convince judges she belongs among the
best. When Marchenko does not want to come, we ask more
nicely. Say please. Write letter. Is politics."

"I guess you must feel awful, then. Inviting Igor to come,
promising he'd be safe, and then him getting killed right in
your own arena!"

Konstantin turned his head to look at Bex. Judging by
the expression on his face, no, the man was actually not too
broken up about the developments.

"It almost sounds," Bex offered, "As if Igor was deliberately lured back to Russia to be killed."

"Ha!" They were back to the realm of one-syllable ex-
clamations. But at least this one, Bex understood.

"You don't think that's what happened?" she pressed.

"There are many, many people who think, inside their
heads, they would like to kill Igor Marchenko."

"Really?" When Bex went fishing, she'd hardly expected to yank up a shark her first cast out. "Like who?"

"Like I, for instance." Konstantin chuckled to himself.

"You?"

"I was the team leader when Marchenko decide he wishes to defect. It is my job to watch the team. I do not watch Marchenko too good. This, when I return to U.S.S.R., is not too good of thing for me. The federation, they do not care how I serve with loyalty for decade before. They only care that Marchenko is defected, and country embarrassed. They punish me. Forbid me from participating in skating competitions. I cannot coach or judge or even come see any competition. They are watching me. I sit home for nearly twenty years before U.S.S.R. is over and I am allowed to return to my sport."

Bex didn't know what to say. "Marchenko did all that to you?"

"I am not only. To me and to many, many others, he did big harm. Marchenko's coach, Alexandr Troika, he is also banned from coaching after Marchenko defects. After U.S.S.R. is over, he tries to come back, also. But it is too late. He has no reputation. No name. No students. And the other athletes, boys and girls who are on World Team with Marchenko. The government is afraid he gave them ideas. Or even maybe they planned to defect together and are waiting for another chance. There are sixteen teammates of Marchenko. Two boys, two girls, three pair team, three dance. All of them are banned forever from international competition. The government takes their passports. They can compete at home, but no international. They are prisoners, yes—that is the correct word? Prisoners. Because Marchenko ruin life for them. So you ask about Russian people who think they want to kill Igor Marchenko? I believe many, many people want to do this."

"Anyone in particular?" Bex figured as long as she was being blatant, she might as well see how far she could go.

Konstantin chuckled again. How lovely that Bex was able to bring the man such joy. It somehow made her entire life more meaningful.

"You think somebody waits twenty-eight years for Marchenko to return to Russia so they may poison him in ice arena?"

"Maybe they weren't just sitting around, waiting? Maybe they were thinking of how they could lure him."

"So you think this killer is me?"

"No!" *Well, not unless you want to confess to something; then I'd be all ears.* "I was just considering all the possibilities."

"You have considered Marchenko's family?"

"His family?" As far as Bex knew, Marchenko's only family was an ex-wife and a ten-year-old daughter, both of whom were back in Connecticut. If either one of them had wanted to kill him, they could have done it locally.

"Marchenko's mother and sister and brother-in-law," Konstantin said.

Oh that family. The one he'd left behind along with his skating teammates. "Why would Igor's family want to see him dead?"

"Because, everything that was done to us in skating, was done even much worse to the family. Government took their apartment. I remember, they have three rooms for themselves, because Marchenko was star athlete. Star athlete's family receives special privileges. After, they are forced in one small room in apartment with another family. Mother is fired from job being engineer in juice factory. Juice factory is good place to work. Much juice to steal. She is given work cleaning streets. Very hard work. Sister and brother-in-law, they are dismissed from University. Shamed at Communist Party meeting in front of friends. Called traitors. Friends are afraid to speak to them. Scared they also will be dismissed from school. If my son or my brother to do this to me, I also think in my head about killing."

"Did you see any of Igor's family at the rink the morning he died?"

"I see no one."

Which, in a way, was even more suspicious. According to Bex's research, Igor had not seen his family in twenty-eight years. At first, they couldn't leave the U.S.S.R., and he couldn't travel to see them. Following *perestroika*, Igor still refused to set foot on Russian soil. But Bex wasn't sure why his family hadn't flown over to see him. Perhaps the unresolved negative feelings there were a bit more intense than your average family's misunderstanding. What other reason could there be for, after twenty-eight years, Igor's mother, sister, and brother-in-law not rushing to greet their prodigal son at the airport and following him around for the duration of his stay in Moscow? And, now that she thought about it, why no response from them about his death? Surely, someone in the press must have tried to contact them. Bex wondered why she hadn't thought of it herself.

"Do you know if Igor was planning to visit his family while he was in town? Or if they were going to come see him?"

"Igor Marchenko," Konstantin replied, "when he see me in arena first day of this competition, he walk right by me, like I am picture hanging on wall. I say to him, 'Igor, you do not remember your old team leader from childhood?' Igor, he turns around, he looks at me for long time, no expression on his face. And then he shrugs. He says, 'No. No, mister, I do not to remember you' and he says this in English. Not in Russian."

Bex made a mental note to ask Sasha the exact Russian translation for the phrase, "Oooh . . . major burn."

But, for now, because she was apparently incapable of remembering even the English phrase for, "Back off," she continued grilling Konstantin, "Do you have any idea where I could find Igor's family? I'd really love to ask them a few questions—"

"Bex!"

She'd never heard her name hollered in an empty ice arena before. It was kind of cool. Every letter seemed to slide off a different wall, like audacious skateboarders on concrete, before slamming into each other in midair to reiterate, "Bex!"

Of course, poetic imagery aside, the disorientation did make it harder for Bex to figure out where she was being beckoned from. She had to look to the right, the left, and down at the ice before realizing that her summons was coming from the tunnel entrance on the side. Where Sasha was now standing, Bex's research binder in one hand.

And holding Amanda Reilly by the elbow with the other.

Five

Sasha looked so darn proud of himself. Bex hated herself for instinctively thinking, "Oh, damn. Why did he do that?"

She realized that Sasha thought he was doing the right thing. Only an hour ago, Bex had been insisting that she desperately needed to speak with Amanda (the words "now, now, now" may even have been bandied about). And now here Amanda was, literally in his grip, and Bex was complaining. And hesitating. But really, there were a couple of good reasons for that.

One, she hadn't finished interrogating Konstantin yet. Not that he seemed all that concerned about the potential abandonment. The federation president was too busy watching his skaters on the ice. Every time one of them missed a jump he grunted in the monosyllabic manner Bex had so recently become familiar with, suggesting that he was otherwise too occupied to care whether Bex actually finished their conversation or not. Bex did notice that, while Brittany

seemed to be having the better day, Konstantin's more involved grunts were saved for his freckle-faced Galina.

Two, Bex did not appreciate Sasha drawing attention to
her . . . oh, what the heck, let's go ahead and call it an investigation—Bex had inadvertently done so many by now,
she might as well give her activities an official title—by
loudly hollering her name and gesticulating wildly in
Amanda's direction. Such actions didn't exactly carry the
subtlety of an Agatha Christie drawing-room revelation. Or
a buzz saw.

Third and most importantly, by clueing Amanda in to the
fact that Bex wished to speak to her, and then giving
Amanda the time it would take Bex to jog all the way down
the two hundred, metal arena stairs to reach them at the side
tunnel entrance, Sasha was ruining Bex's element of surprise. And Bex's element of surprise was her most powerful
weapon. Primarily because she didn't really have any other
ones. It's not as if she had any legal authority to question
these people. Starting with the Silvana Potenza murder of a
year ago, Bex's modus operandi had been to mentally sneer,
"We don't need no stinkin' legal authority" and just go about
blithely questioning people. Until she was told to stop. What
was most strange was that, so far, no one had really told her
to stop.

It was amazing how trivial it proved to get people to talk
to you when you sort of, kind of, but not really implied you
could get them on TV.

Of course, Bex thought ruefully as she sprinted towards
Amanda and Sasha, her usual problem with Mrs. Reilly was
not in getting the proud mom to start talking. It was in getting her to say anything actually useful.

"Mrs. Reilly! Hello!" The flaw in Bex's plan was that, by
running, she had reached Amanda faster than if she'd just
walked, but now she was also too out of breath to ask her
anything of consequence.

"Bex?"

"Yes?" She had to take a deep breath between syllables.

"Why is this Russian boy holding my arm?"

"This is . . ." Another gasp. Bex put her hand on a nearby table to steady herself. "This is Sasha. He's working with me as a translator."

"Yes, I know. We met earlier. Do you need a translator to talk to me, Bex?"

Bex waved her hand nervously in Sasha's direction, fanning her flushed cheeks at the same time. "Please let go of Mrs. Reilly's arm, Sasha."

He promptly did as she asked. But he reminded Amanda, "Bex wishes to speak to you. Please to answer her questions," before pivoting around, giving Bex a covert wink, and walking a respectful distance away from their conversation. He rested his back along the opposing wall, all the while keeping his eyes exclusively on Amanda, lest she decide to bolt and Sasha be needed for the Russian version of a football tackle.

"What a strange young man," Amanda lowered her voice. "I had barely walked in the door before he was standing in front of me. I didn't even see him coming. But he told me it was imperative that you speak to me about something. I was afraid to say no. I thought he might be KGB!"

"No," Bex said lightly. "He's just TV."

The joke either flew straight over Amanda's head, or she didn't think it was much of a joke. All things considered, Bex figured she had a fifty percent chance of being right either way.

"What did you need to talk to me about, Bex?"

Bex looked around. This tunnel, while not the wacky hotbed of activity zooming around the production offices, did have television tech people coming and going, as well as Shura, who popped out of his own office every twenty minutes or so look at everybody with squinty-eyed dissatisfaction (Bex wondered if he and the Russian federation chief ever got together to grunt at each other). Not to mention that both the Russian girls and their coaches were on the ice surface barely a few feet away.

"Maybe we should go somewhere more private," Bex suggested.

"I have nothing to hide," Amanda said.

Bex reached into her pocket and pulled out the check she'd borrowed from Igor's billfold. She turned it around so that Amanda could get a good look.

Amanda got a good look.

Going by clichés, Bex expected Amanda's eyes to grow bigger from the jolt. But, instead, it was her nostrils that actually expanded. She took a deep breath, as if trying to absorb massive amounts of nasal spray. The extra air forced her shoulders back and her chest forward until the bulk of her weight was balanced on her heels. A stiff wind might have knocked her over. Bex was sorely tempted to try it. Just to see if there was any truth in Warner Brothers cartoons.

She almost got her wish.

While Amanda struggled to regain her equilibrium, behind them the Russian girls were getting off the ice. From the sound of it, the entire Russian World Team had come to cheer the girls on at the end of their practice session. Bex recognized several of the male skaters and also the top pair and dance teams that she had worked with at previous competitions as they got out of their arena seats and tromped rink-side. Laughing and chattering in Russian, they blew by Bex and Amanda. Galina joined them. Brittany, Bex noted, did not.

As the others gathered around the bubbly Junior World Champion, handing her a fresh bottle of water and a rag to wipe her blades, Brittany stayed on the ice, pretending not to notice that she was being ignored. Even her own coach, a Russian former world champion, left Brittany the second her practice ended, walking over to say a few words to Galina and Slavic company before heading inside the tunnel. Brittany pretended not to catch that particular slight, either. She simply skated to the barrier and slipped on her Russian team jacket. She leaned over to pick up a water bottle that had been knocked to the floor and took a lengthy sip. When one sip didn't provide ample time for her alleged teammates to clear out, Brittany took another one. Only when they were all gone from the exit, did she skate over and plop down on a bench to begin taking off her skates.

Watching Brittany, Bex couldn't help thinking about the years Igor Marchenko had spent as a member of the American team. Had his ostracism been as brutal? And had the bad feelings continued long after his competitive days were over?

At any other time, Bex might have moseyed on over to ask Brittany for her take on the subject. But she had colder ice to melt at the moment.

Amanda Reilly was still staring, presumably dumb-founded, at the cashier's check in Bex's hand. She waited until the Russians had rowdily blown by them before quietly telling Bex, "Yes. Maybe some privacy is a good idea."

The question, of course, was: where?

Not inside the arena, certainly. Thanks to the hollow acoustics, not only every note of program music and every scrape of blade, but also any word instantly ricocheted around the seats like water swirling down the drain. The only reason Bex had ever risked interviewing Valeri Konstantin in such a wide-open venue was because there had been less people in the arena then, and most of them were focused on the skaters. Now, however, not only had the oc-cupying capacity doubled, with more and more skaters and television personnel filing in, but, with the girls off the ice, a bored passerby was much more likely to delegate a few moments to idle eavesdropping than before.

Bex considered taking Amanda in the back to the pro-duction rooms. Surely, no one would be able to overhear anything in that cacophony of television-making. But, the problem there was, television-making was also very distracting. And Bex needed to be able to focus on every word Amanda said.

Her other options were going back to the official hotel. Not optimal because it would give Amanda plenty of time to conjure up a lying excuse.

She supposed they could duck into a café. But that was not optimal because Russian waiters were scary. When Bex asked for water with lunch, for example, they would point her to a rusty steel faucet sticking out from a far wall and tell her to get it herself.

They could also probably step out onto the street.

Moscow . . . in the winter . . . Nope. Not going to be doing that, either.

And then, Bex had a combination flashback and brainstorm.

Less than a year earlier, her very first foray into the (successful, she should add) sleuthing business had featured a murdered Italian judge. Electrocuted inside the San Francisco World Championship arena's refrigeration room. And one of the main reasons why Bex (and, to be fair, Gil) had instantly suspected the death wasn't on the up and up, was simply because, except for the random technician, no one—really, really *no* one—had any good reason to go into an ice rink's refrigeration room.

Which, naturally, made it a very private meeting spot.

Bex grabbed Amanda by the elbow.

"I have an idea," she said. "Follow me."

As Bex smugly gambled, there wasn't a red velvet rope line waiting to get into the refrigeration room ahead of them. The place was so apparently unpopular, it wasn't even locked. Bex simply turned the knob, threw her entire body weight against the door, pushed, groaned, hacked from the dust whittling her nostrils, put her proverbial back into it, and they were inside. Easy as red caviar blini. Honestly, it was as if the room *wanted* them to break in. Or such was Bex's story and she intended to stick to it should some of President Putin's henchmen burst in and demand to know what she was doing there.

Although Bex could not imagine why anyone would make this even a pit stop on their regular itinerary. At least the room the Italian judge, Silvana Potenza, had died in was filled with extraneous arena material not quite important enough to keep in an easily accessible spot, but not quite useless enough to junk altogether, either. Material like old programs, souvenirs past their sell-by date, broken office furniture that someone honestly did intend to patch up someday. . . .

This Russian counterpart had four pipes running from one wall to the next, one at ceiling level, the lowest barely clearing an inch over Bex's head. The only illumination came from three uncovered windows, each one overlooking a street more lifeless than the previous one. The room smelled like a sweaty pair of shoes soaked in urine and left inside a mousetrap. With the twitching mouse still in it. (The last part was less creative metaphor than an actual sight in the corner.) All of the pipes leaked in a different spot and formed a different Rorschach on the floor. As the floor had seemingly not been swept, dusted, or given any mind to since hemophilia was Russia's greatest health crisis, it meant that Bex and Amanda now treaded in about two inches of dense, black filth. To call the matter dirt or even mud would be to pay it an unwarranted compliment.

Fortunately for their mutual *eeew* factor, both women had more on their minds than tidiness. Also, neither was really into shoe fetishes. Bex had long ago surrendered fashion for comfort. She spent so much 2417 time on her feet, sneakers were the only way to dress. As for Amanda, Bex had never seen her in anything but sensible, synthetic fur-lined, gray boots. Of course, Bex had never seen her anywhere outside of an ice rink.

Amanda looked around. "Didn't Silvana Potenza . . ."

"Yes, yes, let's not dwell on it."

". . . in a room just like . . ."

"I said, let's move on." Bex withdrew Marchenko's check from the pocket into which she'd previously stuffed it and waved in rather theatrically in the air. "You were going to explain this?"

"Th-there is nothing to explain." Amanda did her best to appear defiant and dismissive. The stuttering didn't help.

"Is this your signature on this check?"

"Y-yes."

"This check made out to Igor Marchenko?"

"I guess."

"So, you wrote a check to Igor Marchenko, the coach of your daughter's primary competition, and you think there is nothing to explain?"

"It's none of your business, Bex."

This, certainly, was true. But why in the world should Bex let that stop her? She never had before, after all.

"Okay," Bex said. "Don't explain anything to me. I'll just turn right around, go back to the production offices, mention this to Francis and Diana and let them bring it up on air. Would you prefer that ending to this story?"

In her line of work, Bex made a lot of idle threats to get people to cooperate. She made so many it had gotten to the point where she had forgotten how satisfying it was to actually threaten an act she could deliver. Because, boy, could she deliver this one. All Bex had to do was hint that something odd might be going on in Lian-land, and Francis and Diana (not to mention Gil) would be blabbing it all over their broadcast. Bex figured she didn't need to mention to Amanda at this time that, regardless of what Amanda chose to tell her, odds were good that Bex would be mentioning this development to Francis, Diana, and Gil anyway. It was, after all, exactly what she'd been hired to do.

"Oh, please, don't do that!" Amanda exclaimed.

"Then talk to me. Tell me what's going on."

Amanda took so long to reply, Bex imagined she could hear the floor curdling beneath their feet. Finally, she said, "I wrote Igor Marchenko a check."

"Yes," Bex agreed. "I kind of already knew that much."

Amanda met Bex's eyes for the first time since they'd entered the refrigeration room. "How did you get it, anyway?"

Uhm . . . what sounded better? *Bribing the locals* or *breaking and entering*? Bex skipped right over the whole moral and legal conundrum by deciding to table the debate and just wave her hand around in an unconcerned, authoritative manner. "It's standard procedure when someone dies. Igor was here under the auspices of 24/7, since we're the ones covering and paying for the event, so the police gave us all of his things."

Yeah. There. That sounded good.

It must have, because Amanda just sort of nodded her head vaguely and said, "I am begging you, Bex, please don't tell anyone else about my check to Igor. Lian would be ruined if word got out!"

"Why? People switch coaches all the time. And Igor is much better connected internationally than Gary."

"We weren't," Amanda hedged, "switching coaches. Not exactly."

"Then what was the check for?"

"It was for Igor to coach Lian."

"I see . . ."

"You see, we weren't . . ." Amanda took a deep breath, got a plentiful whiff of the aforementioned urine-soaked sneakers and reconsidered. She made a face, taking short, shallow breaths through her mouth as she huffed and puffed out. "We weren't officially switching coaches. Lian is Gary's top student, so he was obviously a better advocate for her than someone who had a competing skater, like Igor did with Jordan. Plus, Lian has been with Gary for such a long time. We're practically family. . . ."

"And Igor didn't want to take Lian full-time, did he?"

"Not exactly," Amanda conceded.

"So what exactly was he willing to do for her?"

"He was willing to give her some spin lessons. In addition to Gary's coaching. I mean, obviously Lian doesn't need any help with her jumping technique. She's landing triple-triple combinations more frequently than any other woman on the circuit."

"I'm sure that's a surprise to Galina Semenova."

"Oh, Galina . . ." Now it was Amanda's turn to do the patented, dismissive yet authoritative wave. "Galina is a flash in the pan. Sure, she can land the triple-triple—"

"And quadruple," Bex reminded.

"All those jumps now. But she's only fourteen years old. She has the body of a child! When she can still do them at seventeen, like my Lian . . ."

Bex supposed she could have interrupted again to point out that at seventeen, her Lian had the same body as fourteen-year-old Galina. But it wasn't worth the trouble. A word or two from Bex was hardly going to rip Amanda from her delusions. And Bex really wanted to get back to the topic at hand. "So, you were having Igor coach Lian on her spins?"

"Yes. Yes. Like I was saying, Lian doesn't need any more work on her jumps, she's already world class. But the international judges seem to have this obsession with spins. That's all we ever hear about Jordan. Look how beautifully she spins, look at that change of position, look at that speed, look at how long she holds them . . . as if any of that really matters. Oh, and her spirals. The judges seem to prefer Jordan's spirals to Lian's. And her footwork. They think she has better footwork. All of those secondary elements, you know? Still, we decided, well, why not? I suppose Lian could use a little polishing, if that's what the judges really want. Igor was going to help her with all that."

"Okay," Bex said. "That's reasonable. And it happens all the time. You know Jeremy Hunt? He skates at your rink? He's one of Toni Wright's students, but now that he's headed for Nationals, Toni was having him work with Igor on some spins and some footwork, too. A lot of coaches do that. Send their kids to a specialist for a bit. Why are you so set on keeping Lian's work with Igor a secret?"

"Because," Amanda confessed, "it *is* a secret. From Gary."

"Oh." Now it all made sense. "Gary didn't know his top student was getting a little outside polishing."

"It would have just upset him so much. You know the history with him and Igor. They're so competitive, even to this day. I didn't see any reason to make waves."

"If Gary finds out you went to Igor for extra coaching—"

"He'll drop Lian. He won't ever coach her again."

"Which, I guess, would really be a problem for you now that Marchenko is dead. You won't even have a backup."

"It would ruin Lian's entire season! Nationals are only a month away. If Gary were to stop coaching her now . . . it's not enough time to find someone else. And Lian is the favorite to win the U.S. title this year!"

Well, assuming Jordan Ares drops dead, yes, she was.

Bex said, "You were taking a heck of a risk then, going to Igor."

"I love my daughter," Amanda said simply. "I want what's best for her. When we first brought her home from China, she was thirteen months old. But she was the size of a six month old. She could barely sit up. Couldn't stand, definitely couldn't walk or crawl. She would just lay there, her eyes following you around the room. When anyone got near her, her whole face would light up and she'd kick her little arms and legs. But then she would get so overwhelmed, she'd burst into tears. At the orphanage, the babies didn't have much human contact. She had some serious developmental delays. I think it was months before she trusted us enough to try and pull herself up to a standing position while holding on to my fingers. Her legs were so weak. Our pediatrician thought some kind of exercise would help. That's how we ended up at the ice rink. She loved it from the first day, the first moment. As soon as she started skating lessons, she just bloomed. Would you believe she used to be so shy, she couldn't make eye contact when she spoke to people? She barely talked above a whisper. Skating didn't just strengthen her legs. It set her free. It made her a person. Skating makes her so happy, Bex. When it comes to Lian's skating, I can't refuse her anything."

Bex wasn't an idiot. She knew when she was being played.

She also knew when the said playing was particularly effective. Because now, instead of seeing either a potential murder suspect or, at least, a suspect's mother, Bex was seeing Amanda Reilly cradling a sickly, newly adopted Lian—though, disturbingly, sickly, newly adopted Lian was wearing a shiny, tot-sized skating costume.

"Please don't tell anyone about my check to Marchenko," Amanda pleaded. "It will ruin Lian's season. Possibly her entire career. And it won't help anyone. It won't bring Igor Marchenko back to life, and it certainly won't help you find his killer."

Well, now, Bex couldn't be so positive about that. Because, from where she was standing (in filth), it certainly gave an already acrimonious Gary Gold another motive for murder. Not to mention Amanda and Lian Reilly. Just how far would either of them go to keep their clandestine coaching a permanent secret? And, while she was dabbling in the motive game, Bex also contemplated how angry Jordan Ares would feel if she found out her mentor was also helping out the competition.

Bex was about to press Amanda for further details, such as an exact accounting of where she, Gary and Lian were for each minute during the time when Igor was poisoned. She had only gotten as far as asking Amanda, "Speaking of Gary, can you remember, was he the one who put Marchenko's gloves on the heater?"

And Amanda had begun to say that she couldn't recall but, it was possible, since Gary was very meticulous about things being put in their proper place—

When the refrigeration room's door creaked slowly open.

As darkness, filth, and stench didn't traditionally add up to the most popular spot in the arena, Bex and Amanda were understandably surprised to be so rudely interrupted.

But not nearly as surprised as when they both caught sight of the interloper.

Brittany Monroe was standing in the doorway. She'd changed out of her skating costume and now wore her regular clothes, looking even more all-American that she had on the ice, if such a thing were possible. Black jeans, a fluffy cherry sweater with equally fluffy white kittens frolicking across the front, high-top sneakers with Velcro straps.

And, in her hands, she clutched a pair of gold-dyed ladies' figure skates.

Which were most definitely not her own.

Six

$\mathcal{B}ex$ and Amanda stared at Brittany.

Brittany stared back at Bex and Amanda. And she clutched the golden skates to her nonexistent breasts so tightly, it looked like she was trying to force-feed both to the fluffy, white kittens.

At first, the shock of the moment kept all three of them rooted in place. After all, what was more shocking than picking a filthy, disgusting site for privacy, only to learn it was actually the hottest filthy and disgusting site in town?

Brittany was the first to regain her bearings. Still clutching the skates, she spun around and attempted to flee without an explanatory word. Her hasty pirouette spurred Bex into action. When Brittany ran, Bex followed. It was instinct, not a plan. If Brittany hadn't budged, Bex would probably have dumbly done the same.

Now, however, she acted impulsively, slogging noisily through the grime in three not very graceful leaps. Two muddy sneaker prints were left on the discolored concrete right outside the refrigeration room before Bex, with a wild lunge, managed to wrap her fingers around Brittany's wrist. She ended up with a handful of cherry-red sweater fluff, but it was enough to slow the fugitive down. To save the fluffy kittens, Brittany braked in her tracks and tugged on her sweater, forcing Bex to let go. But she stopped running.

Bex stated the obvious. "Those aren't your skates."

Brittany looked down at the golden skates she was cradling in first position. The blades of each skate were digging into her elbows. Eight metal hooks at the ankles had already snagged a few loose cherry threads. She wrinkled her brow, either suffering from temporary amnesia or painfully trying to summon up a good reason to contradict Bex. "Yes, they are."

Then Brittany conceded, "No, they're not."

Bex stated the obvious. "They're Galina's."

This time, Brittany didn't even stop to think. "Yes. They are."

"Are you taking them for a walk?" Bex inquired politely. "Is that a Russian team tradition? Sort of like a wacky initiation?"

While Bex was being sarcastic, she noticed Amanda Reilly trying to casually and unobtrusively sneak away. She was inching against the outer refrigeration wall, looking at neither Bex nor Brittany. If she wasn't presumably afraid of drawing more attention to herself, Bex suspected Amanda would have begun to whistle nonchalantly.

Bex thought about turning around to inform Amanda that she hadn't developed amnesia either, that she could still see her, and that she was *choosing* to let Amanda slink away. But she reconsidered. Let Amanda think Bex was done with her. It would lull her into a false sense of security and might prompt her into making a case-solving error. Or so the theory went. Bex had yet to actually witness it in action.

In any case, she had more immediate chicken kiev to fry.

"Well, Brittany," Bex asked. "What's going on?"

"Nothing."

"Why do you have Galina's skates?"

"I . . . uhm . . . I . . ."

Bex sighed. Why was it, in books, sleuths always had brilliant—sociopathic, but brilliant—nemesis to match wits with. While Bex was up against folks too stupid to even try making up an on-the-ball excuse. Just standing here, Bex could think of several credible lies for Brittany to wriggle with. How about: "She left them behind in the locker room and I'm returning them to her."

Or, "She asked me to take them to the skate sharpener's."

Or, "The Russian Skating Federation is so poor now, the skaters have been told we're going to be sharing boots."

Bex considered sharing any of the above with Brittany. Surely, even a scripted answer would be better than the current, all-vowel stuttering. Especially when the real answer was obvious to anyone with eyes. And a suspicious worldview.

Luckily, Bex fit both bills.

She allowed Brittany's silence to flop about like a newborn's limbs for a few more seconds. Then she got bored. And she accused, "You were going to dump Galina's skates in the refrigeration room.

Brittany stopped trying to talk. And just shrugged. She looked down at the floor. But, for a moment, Bex thought she caught the teen peeking defiantly up at Bex, as though simultaneously embarrassed and proud of her actions.

"Not very sportsmanlike behavior, Britt."

"Who the hell cares?" Even the kittens quivered with indignation. "What about the way she treats me? What about the way they all treat me?"

Bex really did see her point. And, being only a few years older than Brittany, she had no interest in going all "listen to your elders" on her with a lecture about why it was wrong to cheat and steal. To be honest, Bex was less interested in the right and wrong on display here, and more about getting the whole story in case she decided to pitch it as a 24/7 feature for Gil.

"How long has this been going on?" she asked Brittany. "The Russian team dissing you like they did after practice today?"

"Oh, from the start, totally." Brittany's arms dropped to their sides, weighed down by the hardships she'd faced. Or just from carrying the two-pounds-each skates. "My first Russian Nationals, I tried my best to fit in. I brought this Russian phrasebook and I even underlined some words to say to them. But everybody just laughed at me the whole time. Galina, she kept pointing at me, and saying, 'You no here. You no here!' and 'You go home!' "

Obviously. Galina Semenova had also underlined some handy Russian-English phrases to help Brittany fit in.

"Usually, when a Russian skater gets on the ice to compete, all the other team members—and I mean everyone, not just the singles, but the pairs and the dancers, too—they sit in the stands and they clap and they cheer and they stomp their feet. It's so, you know, you're not alone out there, you've got teammates supporting you, so you feel, you know, supported. But, every time I get on the ice, every single, single time, they wait until my name is called and I assume my opening position, and then they all get up, the whole group of them, that's a lot of people, more than a dozen, and they walk out. Just to make sure I see them do it, they always sit where they know I'll be facing, they sit behind the judges. And they make a lot of noise, talking Russian as they go, so everybody hears them, too. They want everybody to know that they're leaving. And I'm just supposed to stand there like an idiot, big smile on my face, because judges need to see that big smile, and I watch them go. Do you know how hard it is to skate after that?"

Bex presumed the answer would be, "Very hard." She was about to comment, but Brittany was on a roll.

"Also, you know what else they do? You know what else?

At all of the banquets after competition, they never sit with me at the Russian table."

"I've been to those banquets," Bex pointed out. "And you're always sitting with the American team."

"Well, I—yes. But that's only because they're my friends and I've known them all since we were kids. I would sit with the Russian team. If they were nicer to me."

"Why do you think they're so hostile to you?" Bex asked, all the while feeling confident she knew the answer perfectly well, but willing to let Brittany surprise her.

"It's because I'm American and they think I'm taking a space on the World Team that should have gone to a Russian girl."

Well, there goes any possibility of surprise.

"But it doesn't make any logical sense," Brittany insisted. "I mean, I'm making their team better, stronger."

"How do you figure?"

"Look, think about it. I had to qualify to earn my spot on the World Team. That means even their own Russian National judges decided I was better—a lot better—than their other Russian girls, right? And Russia wants to send the best team it can to Worlds, right? If I win a medal here or at Worlds or whatever, I win the medal for Russia, not for America, so what difference does it make where I'm from, right?"

"Right," Bex finally responded to her frantic prompt.

"Right. And also, look at it this way, by having me on the team, it encourages the other Russian girls to skate better if they want to beat me, right? I'm like, setting the bar higher for them to reach. And that's only going to make the Russian team stronger in the long run, right?"

"That makes sense in theory," Bex agreed, then subtly flipped the conversation to what she had been wanting to discuss all along. "But, I know that when Igor Marchenko came to the U.S.—"

"Right! This is exactly like Igor Marchenko! Look at

him: he won an Olympic Gold, for Pete's sake. And he did it for America. No way would Gary have been able to do that. Was the USFSA supposed to name a worse skater to the team and give up their gold medal to make Gary happy?"

Considering that Bex often thought of Gary Gold as the Man With One Facial Expression, and that she had as tough of a time imagining him happy as she did unhappy, Bex skipped right over Brittany's hypothetical question to pose a more practical one of her own. "How unhappy was Gary do you think? Was he as unhappy as your Russian teammates? Was he as unhappy as you are now?" Bex indicated the stolen pair of skates Brittany had been planning to do God-knows-what to in the refrigeration room.

"Oh, he was pissed. Everybody still talks about it. I mean, ever since I decided to skate for Russia, all I've been hearing is Gary stories. It's like everybody's got one. My old coach back home, he told me that at the first U.S. Nationals where Gary had to skate against Igor, Gary didn't show up for the medal ceremony. And at the press conferences, he wouldn't look at Igor. My coach said it was like Gary decided to pretend Igor didn't exist, and no one was going to change his mind."

"What about later, when they were coaching at the same rink? Did Gary keep pretending Igor didn't exist?"

"I dunno." Brittany shrugged. "That was like, a million years ago."

A million years ago. Or B.B.B. *Before the Birth of Brittany.* And how could anything that happened B.B.B. possibly be of any importance?

"I'm talking about today." Bex tried to hook Brittany's attention by pretending to return to her favorite subject. "You've seen Marchenko and Gary together at a bunch of competitions. What's their relationship like now?"

"I dunno," Brittany repeated, her eyes beginning to twitch with boredom. She looked to the right. She looked to the left. She sighed. She did everything but tap her foot impatiently. "Why don't you, like, ask him yourself?"

In a single move, Brittany managed to jut her chin in the direction of the side door, where Gary Gold was currently standing, and swing both arms behind her back, so that the purloined skates might be hidden from view.

His hand on the knob, Gary was dressed in knee-high furlined boots, a gray, woolen hat, brown leather gloves, and a black, artic-quality parka with attached hood. Bex's superior research skills suggested the gentleman was on his way outside.

And now she had a choice. Either drop the skater in the hand to pursue a coach in the bush, or let Gary go and continue cross-examining Brittany.

Bex decided that pumping a bored Brittany for details about the Marchenko/Gary relationship couldn't possibly be as helpful as asking Gary himself. And so, with a stern glare in Brittany's direction that Bex hoped conveyed the message, "You'd better return those skates to Galina, asap, and never let me catch you engaging in such foolishness, again, young lady," Bex let Brittany off the hook.

"Gary!" she yelled, even as the object of her yelp had already opened the door and taken a pioneering step outside.

He paused, half in–half out the door, and gazed at Bex expectantly. Though, to be honest, Gary was always gazing at people expectantly; this was nothing personal. The man possessed a perpetual air of waiting for someone—anyone!—to articulate something interesting. And then of being bitterly disappointed.

While other coaches taught their students with jokes and a buddy-buddy air, Gary Gold preferred to expound from up high. He gave the impression of looking down at his students, even when they were, in fact, taller than him.

With Bex, though, this wasn't an issue. She barely reached up to his breastbone. Gary's competitive bio may have listed him as five foot, nine inches tall. But, he stood so darn straight, Bex could have sworn the man was an even six feet if he was an inch.

He looked down at Bex now, noting the muddy footprints her frantic scurrying left on the concrete floor, and radiated disapproval.

"May I help you, Miss Levy?"

Miss. It was always *Miss* with him. Bex bet he even called the Gloria Steinem magazine that.

"I wanted to talk to you." She was at the door. The wind blowing in slapped her upside the head and didn't stop to apologize.

"I am on my way out, Miss Levy."

"In this weather?" The morning frost had turned into noontime snowflakes. In Moscow, the snowflakes didn't gently waft from the sky like Currier & Ives angel kisses. They vomited straight down, like heat-seeking missiles determined to eradicate any suggestion of warmth.

Gary smiled. He performed the act so rarely, Bex didn't recognize it at first. But no, that seemed to be genuine amusement in his eyes.

"The street seems full of natives." He indicated the bundled up Russian swarm swerving to avoid the still-open door and shooting him the evil eye for being forced to do so. "I hardly think we're in any danger from the elements."

"Where are you going?" Bex asked stupidly, temporarily stumped for anything more clever she could say to keep him talking to her.

"For a constitutional."

"You mean a walk?"

Ah, and there was that world-famous expression of disappointment, right on schedule. "Yes, Miss Levy. I am going for a walk."

"Can I come with you?"

"In this weather?" he asked, deadpan. But Bex had to believe there was mocking—of her, of course—involved.

"Sure." Bex stepped over the threshold, closing the arena

door behind them, both to avoid any more angry swerving and cursing Russians, and to keep Gary from escaping. "I don't think we're in any danger from the elements."

Although, maybe she was wrong about that. For, while Gary could boast about taking a constitutional in a military-strength snowstorm while wearing snow boots, thick gloves and a hooded parka, Bex was dressed only in the down-jacket and sneakers she'd donned for braving the rink. And she hadn't exactly been overheating in them as it was.

Bex reached into her right pocket, happy to find the gloves she'd packed in earlier still there, and hurriedly slipped them on. The non-fur-lined, more-fall-than-winter pair helped a bit. But she was still hatless. The kamikaze snowflakes pricked her ears, then saw her open neck and pounced, en mass. Bex stuffed her ponytail down the back of her jacket, and pretended that was enough.

"So?" If her teeth were already chattering, it couldn't possibly portend comfort to come. They hadn't even stepped out from the shelter of the arena, yet. Oh, the things she did for . . . Bex was too cold to recall at the moment. "Where are we going?"

"To experience Moscow!" Gary proclaimed with a great deal more enthusiasm than she'd ever heard him give to any-thing, including a student winning Nationals. "It truly flab-bergasts me how many skaters travel the world, stopping at some of the most beautiful and storied places on the globe—Moscow, Paris, Tokyo, Istanbul—and never take the time to so much as poke their noses outdoors. When else will they get the chance to immerse themselves in another culture, an-other language, an utterly different way of life. It's shock-ing. Shocking! Don't you think, Miss Levy?"

So far, on this trip, Bex had seen her hotel room, the arena, the police station, and the gray road from the hotel to the police station to the arena.

"Shocking," Bex agreed.

They crossed the street, ducking a fleet of snub-nosed

cars that looked as if a giant hand were squishing them from above. On either side of them tromped a hoard of snow-covered, fur-clad Muscovites, each wrapped up so thoroughly in the former pelts of gray rabbits, or russet foxes, or even sleek, black minks it was impossible to tell the men from the women, except that the women sometimes wore colorful headscarves underneath their hats, and the men made do with earflaps that tied beneath their chins. Bex supposed she could have also made her gender guesses based on footwear, but with two inches of snow already skidding on the ground and more retching each minute, it looked like everybody was wearing slippers made of chilled whipped cream.

"You know," Bex ventured as she spat a snowflake from her tongue. "We're not going to see too much of Moscow with this kind of zero-visibility."

She'd been hoping Gary would reply with, "Of course, Bex! You are absolutely right. I will save my sight-seeing for another time and promptly return to the arena—no, better, the hotel bar, where we shall both warm up while I regale you in detail with how I single-handedly murdered one Igor Marchenko. And why. No, I don't mind if you bring your tape recorder. Bring an entire camera crew if you'd like!"

But, of course, what he really said was, "You think so, do you?"

"Uhm . . . yeah. I can hardly see anything. I mean, I know Moscow's supposed to have this fantastic architecture and everything, but—"

"There is more to a city, to a culture, than architecture."

"Well, yes, I know that, but it's not like you and I are going to be chatting with the local citizenry, either. Everyone's running like crazy to get in out of the snow."

Hint. Hint, hint, hint.

"Everyone?" Gary asked. He looked at Bex in that way teachers have when they know you have the wrong answer, you know you have the wrong answer, and you both know neither one of you is budging from the spot until you come up with the right one.

"Almost everybody," Bex insisted. "Well, except for those people . . ."

She indicated the building directly across from the arena. Because of an awning, the sidewalk in front of what seemed to be a multi-story apartment residence boasted about two feet free of the most direct snow. Slush had been kicked into the vicinity and passing buses periodically sloshed up a crackling puddle, but no new snow was falling directly on the half-dozen or so people huddling beneath the first floor windows. They appeared to be street-vendors of some sort. Each had a tablecloth, kerchief, or at least a sack spread out in front of them. One woman was hawking wooden, hand-illustrated stacking dolls, ranging from rosy-cheeked Russian maidens to deposed Soviet premiers and American presidents. Another man displayed bottles of colorful potions in a hand-carved wooden case, while a third featured stacks of silver forks, spoons, serving platters and authentic samovars. On the very edge, pointedly separate from the others, a dark-skinned couple, possibly Gypsies judging by the several golden hoops in each ear, waved wooden, pencil-length sticks with bright red sugar candy in the shape of roosters, horses and bears perched on top. Several of the roosters, horses, and bears' tails and ears were already crumbling.

Gary looked at Bex expectantly. "Rather makes the whole chatting with the locals process seem extraneous, does it not, Miss Levy? Most people's stories are right there for everyone to see. No language barrier. No political spin."

"This is what you do?" Bex asked. "You walk around and look at people?"

"Do you know of a better way to acquaint yourself with a civilization? Just look at them. Why do you suppose that they, unlike everyone else, are not hurrying to get in out of the snow?"

"They're selling things." Bex stated the obvious, knowing that she was stating the obvious, and knowing that Gary knew she was stating the obvious, but also knowing that he wanted her to say it, anyway. "They're poor. They can't leave."

"We see this at every place we go. Even in the United States. Here we all come, descending on some luxury hotel or arena, dragging our stuffed suitcases full of clothes, complaining of actual starvation when room service is more than twenty minutes coming, dissolving into hysterics over a judge's mark or a slipped edge. As if any of this actually matters. As if anyone outside of the arena even cares what went on inside it. As if any of this were actually life or death."

That, Bex thought, was an opening if she ever heard one.

They'd made a left and were now walking away from the frozen, metaphor-rich street vendors, and towards a corner dotted with various stores. Electronics, magazines, groceries, a butcher shop. It all looked perfectly normal and perfectly Western. That is, until a heavy-set woman exited the butcher shop, dressed in the white coat and chef-like hat of an employee, grunted loudly and bent over at the edge of the sidewalk. In her hand was a blood-stained butcher knife. With practiced speed, she scraped first one side of the knife, then the other, against the ground; either cleaning it or sharpening it, Bex couldn't be sure. Bits of animal fat plopped into the puddle, floating amidst the ice chips and lost leaves. The woman looked at her knife, grimly satisfied, and marched back inside.

Bex said, "Wow . . ." Her mind temporarily going blank.

Luckily, Gary remembered the purpose of her seemingly innocent tag-along, even when Bex did not. He guessed: "You wished to speak to me about Igor."

Yes. Yes, she had. It had been Bex's only reason for stepping outside. And now, thanks to the butcher-woman and her dirty or dull knife, she had actually forgotten for a minute. Clearly, Bex was having a life-changing cultural expence.

But she could always have one of those later.

Cross-examining a witness always came first.

"You had a motive for killing Igor," Bex said simply. She figured that trying to outsmart someone who was obviously smarter than she was would be the definition of stupid. So she might as well play stupid in the hope that it would prove the wiser option. In case anyone ever wondered, yes, Bex could make her own head hurt simply by thinking.

Gary, on the other hand, appeared utterly nonplussed. Head upright, gloved hands stuffed into his pockets, eyes peering out from beneath his furry hat, he didn't even break stride as he agreed, "Of course, I did, that much is obvious."

"Did you kill him?"

"Don't be absurd."

"You hated him."

"No. No, I did not."

"He won the National title you thought was yours."

"It *was* mine. The title is Senior Men's Champion of the United States. What logic is it to have the winner be a non–United States citizen? It's default by definition."

Gary stopped by a wooden booth the color of limes, the size of an outhouse. It stood in the middle of the street and, as far as Bex could tell, served no purpose. But then, Gary fished around in his pocket, pulled out a dull gold three-kopek piece and dropped it in a slot by Bex's ear. He pushed a button and, from a bread-box–sized window over on his side of the presumed outhouse, coughed an intermittent stream of urine-colored water. It fired several blasts into a film-coated glass, culminating with a rim of foam.

Gary reached for the glass, tilted it in Bex's direction so she could see the inside, and, after informing her, "It's sugared syrup water," proceeded to drink the dubious concoction down in a single gulp. "Three kopeks for the syrup. It's the best deal on the continent!" Gary wiped his lips by daintily pressing his right thumb and pointer-finger along the edges of his mouth. He replaced the community glass back onto its perch, and, once again without missing a stroke, educated Bex: "Being permitted to compete at the U.S. Nationals was not Igor's fault. The USFSA allowed him to do it. My remonstration was never with him. It was with the association."

Well. That was a detail no one had bothered to share with Bex. "And your taking your medal off on the stand . . ."

"The association handed the medals out. I was protesting their actions. Perfectly legitimate political protest."

"I heard you wouldn't talk to Igor during press conferences."

"Why should I speak to Igor during press conferences? At a press conference, the media asks the questions and the athletes answer them. Igor was never a member of the media, what reason did I have to address him?"

"So you didn't hate him?"

"I did not like him," Gary offered. "But I also did not kill him."

"Do you have any idea who might have?"

"The Russians." There wasn't a second of hesitation in Gary's voice. "Have you investigated the Russians?"

"Actually, I have. I spoke to Valeri Konstantin. He said that Igor's defection was so long ago; no one still carries a grudge."

"Igor's defection happened almost exactly as many years ago as his usurpation of the National title. If my motive is still valid, why would their motive not be?"

See? Bex knew the man was smarter than she was. Leave it to Gary Gold to take her play-stupid strategy and make her feel . . . stupid.

"How much do you know about Russian history, Miss Levy?"

Okay, now he's just showing off.

"Not much," Bex admitted.

"There once was a Georgian fellow by the name of Josef Stalin. He joined the Social Democratic Party in 1899. He switched to the Bolsheviks in 1903. He was arrested and exiled to Siberia numerous times, the final incarceration lasting from 1913 until 1917 and the October Revolution. He became the general secretary of the party in 1922. In 1927, he deported various political opponents. In 1929, he deported even more people, entire communities of Poles, Chechens, Tatars, and the like. From 1934 to 1939, he moved on to the mass murder of anyone who didn't agree with him or anyone he thought might challenge his power. By the time he died in 1953, he was making plans to deport the Soviet Union's Jews . . ."

Bex nodded sagely while completely missing his point.

"Over fifty years, Miss Levy. Fifty years, and he still was not done massacring the country to fit his own needs. He did not do it quickly. He understood that if you try to move too quickly, you have a revolt on your hands. He did it gradually. A man, a group, a race at a time. These people know how to wait. It's what they're best at. They waited out the Mongols, they waited out the Czars, they waited out the Communists. Dozens of years of waiting. Hundreds of years of waiting. Igor Marchenko betrayed his country less than thirty years ago. That's not a very long wait, at all."

Well, sure, not when you put it that way . . .

Bex wished she had something pithy and relevant to add to his lecture, but, as she did not, she went with the banal: "How did you learn so much about Russian history?"

"Don't you know?"

"Know what?"

"It wasn't in your research?"

She could see that he was mocking her now (again), and she could see that he was getting a kick out of it. The only thing Bex couldn't see, was his point. "I'm sorry, Gary, I don't know what you're talking about."

"You do not know that I am Brittany Monroe?"

The overwhelming image of Gary dressed up in Brittany's fluffy kitty sweater rendered Bex effectively speechless. Which seemed to have been Gary's goal.

He went on, "Well, I could have been, anyway. Technically, I am more Russian that she is. My mother was born in Kiev. It was the U.S.S.R., then, so I could have claimed citizenship. Is it not ironic? I would have had a more legitimate case to enter the Soviet Nationals than Igor did to compete in the United States."

"Why didn't you?" Bex asked flippantly. "Might have taught Igor a lesson!"

But Gary failed to see the humor in her query. Without a word to Bex, he turned on his heel and began walking back towards to the arena.

"Wait!" She had to trot to keep up with him. "I'm sorry!"

She had no idea for what, but she really was sorry.

Mostly because she'd spent the past half-hour in the freezing cold talking about every issue under the sun except the one she really needed addressed.

Gary kept walking. But, without looking at Bex, he snapped, "I have no use for the Soviet Union. No use for the Russians, for the Ukrainians. My mother was a little girl when the war began. World War Two. The Nazis came, her neighbors tripped over each other telling the Germans where they could find their Jews. Her family was taken away and shot. She only survived because a neighbor grabbed her by the back of her dress when she was running into the courtyard after her parents, grabbed her by the back of her dress and pulled her, kicking and crying, into their apartment. They hid her under the bed until the Nazis left the courtyard. And then they turned her out into the street to fend for herself. But they saved her life. It was something."

He slowed his pace. Bex caught up to him. They walked in silence for a few moments. The arena was already in sight when Gary asked, "You genuinely think that I killed Igor?"

Choosing her words with great care, Bex said, "Igor was

killed by a homeopathic poison in his gloves. The poison was probably liquid. Whoever poured it into Igor's gloves also had to dry them, so Igor wouldn't notice until it was too late. Shura, he's the arena manager, he said he saw you putting Igor's gloves on the heater while Igor was by the ice, coaching Jordan."

"I might have done it," Gary said.

For a moment, Bex thought he was confessing. But then, she realized he simply meant . . .

"I might have put Igor's gloves on the heater," Gary continued. "I absolutely cannot stand slatternly behavior. Children, today . . . they have no respect. It is bad enough when, at their own rinks, they throw their belongings on the floor, willy-nilly, waiting for Mummy to come clean up after them. But when we are all guests in someone else's country, I absolutely will not stand for flinging your belongings about like common riffraff. I have made it a habit to pick up such objects and restore some semblance of order. Considering the level of respect that Igor held for his country of birth, I have no difficulty believing that he treated the arena like his own personal garbage bin.

"If that was the case, it's quite conceivable that I picked up his gloves and, if I found them wet, laid them on the heater to dry. After all, I would have no way of knowing whose gloves they were. And, even if I did, I doubt that would have altered my instincts."

"Is it possible it wasn't Igor, but the killer who dropped his gloves on the floor?" Bex asked. "Like, maybe he didn't want to get any of the poison on himself, so he didn't want to hold them any longer than he absolutely had to?"

"It's a valid theory," Gary replied. "Not one I have anything to contribute to, but it is valid."

Was he actually complimenting her intelligence? Her logic? Bex couldn't tell. All she knew was, suddenly, Gary wasn't looking at her as if 24/7's only researcher was coated in a shell of stupid. And, coming from him, that was a major victory.

Bex wished she could take a minute to bask in the praise-like emotion. But, alas, a researcher's work was never done.

Especially since, as Gary and Bex approached the arena's main doors, both saw an ambulance loading a pair of bodies onto stretchers.

Seven

Bex ran towards the ambulance, temporarily forgetting her latest potential murder suspect and cursing her bad luck. How dare someone get hurt while Bex was away from the arena? Gil would have Bex's head for this! It was bad enough they probably had no footage of the accident (Gil could never understand why Bex didn't psychically predict these things and have a crew set to tape any sort of tumble before it happened), but now, Bex wouldn't be able to do her first-hand-account write-up for Gil and have it on his desk ten minutes ago! This was a calamity. A true tragedy.

And, oh, yeah, it looked like someone had gotten hurt, too.

Bex reached the ambulance as the second stretcher was being loaded up. She'd been too far away before to see who was on it, and now, a paramedic blocked her way. Bex craned her neck for a peek, but all she saw was two pairs of seemingly female feet. Bex knew they were skater appendages thanks to the bleeding calluses on the toes of one, and the protruding bone spurs on the arches of another.

And then, like a miracle, Sasha appeared in front of Bex.

"It is alright." Sasha grabbed Bex by both elbows so that she was looking at him, head-on. "I saw this what happened. I write everything down for you."

She wanted to kiss him. She could have, too. They were facing each other at just the right angle. His head was directly above hers, his arms were more or less in the proper position, and, best of all, he came bearing news that made Bex awesomely and deliriously happy. All the stars were perfectly aligned and might never be so again. Bex could have kissed him, and it wouldn't have even seemed that inappropriate.

Except that, in that moment, curiosity won out over all other instincts. She turned her head away, scattering the aforementioned stars out of their possibly once-in-a-lifetime alignment to excitedly ask, "Who is it?"

"Galina Semenova and Brittany Monroe."

Darn. Bex had been hoping for at least one American. The U.S. public preferred the spilled blood to gush from someone they might bump into on the street one day. Well, maybe they could make do with promoting Brittany's injury, if they spun it carefully.

"What happened?"

"Brittany and Galina, they to have a collision on each other."

"Accidental or deliberate?" Most elite skaters were pretty good at practicing their programs while peering over to keep from crashing into another athlete. But, collisions did still happen. Especially when one—or both—parties really wanted them to.

"Deliberate, I believe."

"Really?" This could be good. The U.S. viewing public might be made to care about non-American blood-spilling if they were also told it had been a deliberate grudge match. Bex could already see her tag line: "This time, it's personal."

She asked, "Who crashed in to whom?"

"Galina's hand hits Brittany's face and makes blood."

Even better! A split lip was much more cinematic than a bruised shin. Much more visceral. And this was beginning to sound like a good old-fashioned smack-down!

"And Galina was hurt, too? I saw two stretchers outside."

"Yes. Brittany, she hits Galina in the stomach with her knee."

"Accidentally or on purpose?"

"Definitely with purpose."

"This is great!" Bex could no longer contain her enthusiasm. "Do you know if one of our 24/7 cameramen was shooting the practice? If we've got footage of this, my life is made!"

"Oh, no," Sasha said. "I do not believe so. The collision, you see, it did not take the place on the ice. The collision, it to takes place in front of ladies' changing room."

"Galina just went off and smacked Brittany?" Bex clarified in the taxi on their way to the hospital Sasha described as "best in the city—they are very lucky to be taken there."

"Galina just walked up and hit Brittany across the face?"

"Yes. This is what happened. And then Brittany to hit her back. And Galina, she push Brittany hard, and Brittany swing her skate bag at Galina's head and then—"

"Do you have any idea why?"

"Galina, she is screaming to Brittany about her skates. She says, 'You take my skates from me, you female dog!' "

Ah. Yes. That would do the trick.

Bex filled Sasha in on her earlier encounter with the footwear-napper. Then, returning to the story Gil expected to be the centerpiece of their coverage, she said, "You know, when I hear about Brittany and Galina going at it, I don't find it hard at all to imagine that Gary hated Igor enough to kill him."

"Can you to prove this?" Sasha asked.

Bex was wondering the same thing herself

They got out of the cab in front of the Central Hospital's main entrance. While Sasha sprinkled the necessary Russian words—and bribes—to get them inside, Bex stood out of the way, and studied the ambiance. She wasn't surprised to see that the admission area was painted in mosaic chips of gray, offered no windows, and stood illuminated by a single, low-wattage lamp atop a pile of books next to the black, rotary phone. She wasn't surprised to see the medical staff outfitted exactly like the butcher-woman had been, in a white coat and matching chefs hat. What did startle Bex somewhat was the spectacle of an orange tabby cat strolling out from the swinging doors that, Bex presumed, led to the actual wards. Kitty casually strolled over to the admission desk where, Bex just noticed, there stood a dark blue metal saucer, half filled with what might have been a chewed-up sardine. Or the last remnants of a patient. It wasn't bright enough inside the waiting area to make out the exact details clearly. After Bex had watched Kitty take a few bites of the concoction, lazily lick her paw, then head back towards the wards, she could only hope it was the former.

"We have permission." Sasha took Bex by the elbow. "Let us go in now." He led her in the same direction as the cat.

They walked down a hallway smelling of gauze, camphor, and disinfectant. The floor had been recently washed. Bex noticed the streaks, as well as the dirty buckets and mops still standing in the corner.

"This is the best hospital in the city?" she whispered to Sasha.

He nodded fervently, and looked surprised that she'd asked the question.

Brittany, however, did not appear to share Sasha's lofty

opinion. Or so they were led to deduce based on her screams ricocheting down the hall.

"If you think I'm letting you near me with that needle, you're insane!" Russia's potential sweetheart howled in Ohio-English. "I'm not staying in this disgusting snake pit for another minute! I'm an American. You get it? An American? Get your leeches away from me!"

By the time Bex and Sasha got there, Brittany was standing by the examining room door, her back towards the hallway, holding a wooden stool nearly half her size and waving it in front a befuddled, white-clad nurse, who was clutching a syringe in her right hand. Except for the handprint-shaped bruise running from the tip of her lips to just under her left eye, Brittany certainly appeared none the worse for wear.

She caught sight of Sasha and commanded, "Tell her I am not getting any kind of shot from this place. I know what goes on inside Russian hospitals, don't think I don't. I read all about how they use disposable needles here over and over again until everybody gets AIDS or worse. She's not touching me. Nobody here is."

Sasha said something in Russian to the nurse. The nurse said something back and waved the syringe emphatically. Brittany refused to put down her stool.

Sasha said, "She says, the shot, it is for tetanus, if you were cut by some metal."

"Tell her I got a tetanus shot two years ago, when I fell down during practice and another kid skated over my hand and sliced it open. Those things are good for ten years."

Sasha dutifully translated. The nurse tried to press her point.

"No!" Brittany barked, and jabbed the stool at her again, lion-tamer style.

Sasha, without saying a word, reached over, yanked it out of her hand and put it behind his back. For a moment, Brittany looked like she was about to make a lunge for it. But the look on Sasha's face suggested he wouldn't advise it.

The nurse said a few more things only Sasha understood, but, in the end, she left the three of them alone and exited the room. Bex could only imagine what stories she'd be telling her family over dinner about crazy Americans.

"Thanks," Brittany told Sasha, perfunctorily. Then launched straight back into talking about herself "Can you believe they put me on the same ambulance as Galina? I mean, I'm the victim here, and I had to stare at that ugly, Ronald McDonald mug of hers the whole way over."

"Why did you even call an ambulance?" Bex asked. "You don't seem that badly hurt. And you've certainly made your opinion about Russian hospitals crystal-clear."

"I didn't call the ambulance. I think someone from the arena did. Galina was lying on the floor, clutching her stomach, all moaning and groaning. Oh, look, look at me, I'm hurt, boo-hoo, pity me, let me win, since that's the only way I'm ever going to. She's such a faker. I didn't even hit her that hard. There's hardly anything in my bag to do damage with. I wasn't going to let her hog the spotlight and get the sympathy. When the ambulance came, I told the paramedics they had to take me, too. Fair is fair."

Bex asked, "I thought I told you to put her skates back where you got them."

"I did! I did it right after you took off chasing Gary Gold. They were back in her bag; she'd have never known the difference. If that creepy Shura guy hadn't told her. I guess he saw me taking the skates out. Or putting them back in, either one. I bet he's got a peephole drilled into the girl's changing room, or something. He told Galina I took her skates. Though I don't know what the big deal is—I put them back, didn't I? Didn't do anything to them; though I could have, you know. I totally could have, like, dug nicks in her blades and let her break her stupid neck landing one of those, 'Oh, I think I'm so much better than everyone else quadruple jumps.'"

"Did you try to apologize?" Bex asked.

"I didn't get a chance! Little bitch right-hooked me the second I stepped out of the changing room. She smacked my face, she pulled my hair, and that bastard, Shura, just stood there, laughing at me. He was the nearest guy there, and he didn't try to stop her or anything. He just watched and laughed. And then he called me 'American shit.' Can you believe it? Where does he get off? Dude is a glorified janitor and he's calling me names! Besides, I'm on the Russian team. I'm Russian. Why doesn't anybody get that? I'm just as good as they are. Why does everyone hate me so much?"

And then, Brittany Monroe, Russian National Champion, did the last thing Bex ever expected. She burst into tears.

Bex and Sasha got Brittany calmed down and into a taxi returning her to the hotel before they ventured back inside the hospital. They stepped over the cat who was now chasing a loose bit of plastic foam down the hall, and went looking for Galina. They found her still lying on the same stretcher she'd come in on. That stretcher was parked outside an examination room. The examination room was open. If they were so inclined, all three of them could have peeked inside and observed the attending doctor press his stethoscope against a wheezing, elderly woman's chest. As she sat wearily on the examining table. Completely topless and facing the door.

Apparently, Bex was the only member of the group who found this peculiar.

She looked down at Galina. The elfin girl had a few scratches on her face, as well as one her forearms. She had both arms wrapped around her stomach, elbows jutting up towards the ceiling. She didn't look so much in pain, as pissed off

She too began talking the instant she spied Bex and Sasha. The torrent of Russian flooded them both, then bounced off Bex's ears like a vending-machine rubber ball.

"Galina, she says that Brittany is crazy lunatic person," Sasha tried to translate, though Galina had yet to stop talking. "She says she should to be arrested and deported. And shot, too."

"Ask her if she wants to give her side of the story." Gil would demand that, and, even though Bex suspected she already knew what Galina would have to say, she figured she should do things officially, nonetheless.

"She says that her statement is Brittany Monroe is crazy lunatic person."

"Anything else?"

"She should be arrested and deported and—"

"Shot, yes, I know."

"No. Galina say she will be content if Brittany only is forbidden from competing in Russian Nationals. This is as good as shooting, she says."

Bex idly wondered if Gary Gold might have once said the same thing about his own nemesis. And whether, years down the line, he changed his mind and decided, no, you know what, I'd actually rather have him dead, after all.

"Ask her if she needs anything," Bex offered. She didn't want it to seem like she was taking sides, but while Brittany could always retreat to America for treatment of any lingering injuries that might still come up (or, at the very least, use American dollars to buy herself superior care), Galina, Bex guessed, was at the mercy of this first-rate health facility. And Bex did not want to see her end up as Kitty's supper.

Sasha translated Bex's query. Galina looked at her suspiciously, shook her head, and rattled off some incomprehensible, yet still dismissive patter.

"She to says she does not need any help from you. If she is hurt badly, she knows where to get what medicine she needs."

Bex, recalling what Brittany had screamed in her hysteria about AIDS-infected needles, wished she shared Galina's optimism.

"Well, is she sure she doesn't want—"

"Galina says, you do not worry about her. Even if hospital not have the medicine that she needs, she is used to this and she can do like everyone, and use good, people's . . . no, folk, I think they are called folk, remedies. She says there is a man who sits outside of skating arena who sell medical potions that she buys from all the time, when she needs something for pain or injury or illness."

Bex froze. She knew the man Galina was talking about. Gary had pointed him out to Bex during their frosty walkabout. But she hadn't made the connection until now. The man outside the arena, the one with the little bottles of colorful potions. He sold folk remedies. Homeopathic medicine.

Like the kind that had killed Igor Marchenko.

It didn't matter how fast Bex willed or Sasha pleasantly bribed the cab to return to the arena. No cab could travel back to the time when the Holistic Healing Man Bex was now so desperately seeking was still planted in the cold; several colorful, stacking dolls on one side, shunned Gypsies on the other. Where the heck was that guy? He could sit hawking his wares in the middle of a snowstorm but what, at sundown he turned into a pumpkin? Bex cursed herself for not having made the connection sooner. Obviously, Igor's killer had to get his poison somewhere. Finding out who'd purchased a dose of homeopathic digitalis in the past few days while in the vicinity of the arena sure would help Bex narrow down who might have poured it into Igor Marchenko's gloves.

She considered going over to cross-examine to the Gypsies, who were still sitting in the same spot, but Bex didn't want to tip her hand or reveal her agenda. So, dejected, she planted Sasha outside the arena to keep watch and gave him strict orders to come get her immediately in case Holistic Healing Man returned.

And then she returned to the 24/7 offices feeling as if the entire day had been a waste. Yes, she now knew a lot more things. But none of them were relevant or even useful. Bex sat down at her designated desklike structure—actually a standing iron board—and proceeded to type up her report about the Galina/Brittany fracas. She tried to make it as dramatic as possible for Gil, to justify her existence as a researcher, yet not so dramatic that, when Francis and Diana added their own gloss of hyperbole, the whole thing began to sound like there had been pistols at dawn and life-threatening injuries involved. Most importantly, Bex tried not to take sides, knowing that 24/7 would do that perfectly well on its own. Brittany, with her Russian citizenship or not, would be painted the heroine, Galina the groundless instigator. Gil insisted that every story needed someone that people could root for, and someone to hiss at. Curious to see if this was a relatively new phenomenon, Bex took a break from writing her report and went on-line. She managed to locate some newspaper accounts from Igor's and Gary's competitive days. She noticed, much to her chagrin, that a similar ethos seemed to have prevailed even thirty years ago. Only this time, the tables were turned, and plucky Russian refugee Igor was deemed the hero, while all-American Gary Gold was the villain (though, to be fair, Gary's being from New York branded him a kind of foreigner even before the Marchenko chronicle came up). All because Gary'd had the audacity to publicly ask why Igor, already the product of free training from the mighty Soviet sports machine, should now receive even more money and resources from the United States Figure Skating Association—money and resources ostensibly raised and donated to train needy American skaters.

For his reasonable questions, Gary was designated green-eyed and petty by the media. Reporter after reporter wrote

how obviously and visibly jealous Gary was that Igor had
snuck in and won the title Gary selfishly assumed would be
just given to him, like a coronation. (They pretty much ignored the fact that Gary had won said title fair and square
the previous year. Considering it took him four years in senior men's competition to make it onto the podium, Bex
doubted Gary expected anything to just be handed to him.)

But a story had to be told and a mythos created. So Igor
was good, Gary was bad, no questions asked. It interested
Bex to note that, in stories written fifteen, even twenty years
after the initial rivalry had faded from public consciousness,
sports reporters who couldn't have been around when it all
started still picked up on old gossip. When writing about
Lian Reilly versus Jordan Ares, for example, they dragged
out the same chestnuts about Gary's inferiority complex
where Igor Marchenko was concerned and his supposed obsession with one day, finally "beating" the Russian. Any
way he could.

And speaking of Lian Reilly . . . that reminded Bex. She
had gotten so distracted with Brittany and Galina and Holistic Healing Man that she had nearly forgotten that, on the
last exciting episode of "Who Iced Our Coach?" she'd left
Amanda claiming the check Bex found in Igor's possession
was payment for the Russian secretly coaching Lian. But, so
far, Bex only had Amanda's word for that. It would be nice
to get a little confirmation.

A notice on the assignment board indicated that a camera
crew was currently out with Lian Reilly and her mother,
filming America's wannabe sweetheart as she attended the
world famous Bolshoi Ballet.

Bex had always wanted to see the Bolshoi Ballet.

Well, at least she did now.

She popped her latest research report into Gil's in box,
grateful that he was away from his own ironing board and
thus not available to ask Bex questions that could be an-

swered simply by reading the report, and headed outside to check on Sasha's vigil.

After determining that no news, in this case, was no news, Bex took pity on her poor runner—it was his first day in big-time, professional television, after all—and told Sasha he could go home. She would handle the rest of the evening's work on her own.

To Bex's surprise, he looked somewhat disappointed by her dismissal. Bex was about to ask him why. After all, she asked everyone else personal details about their lives. It was her job, wasn't it? So why should Sasha be any different?

Except that, for some reason, he was. Bex didn't refrain from asking Sasha anything personal out of respect for his privacy. Rather, she refrained because she knew Sasha would give her an honest answer. And she just was not ready to know or understand him any better right now. The absent mother, the drunk father, the orphanage, his dreams of media success, all those details were already too personal, too . . . real. Bex thrived better in the land of glib. The land where one's biggest crisis was a loose sequin falling off a costume and snagging a skate blade. Where even knock-down, drag-out fistfights were triggered by a hunger for medals and not actual, you know . . . hunger.

"Good night to you, then," Sasha said as politely as he'd said everything else that day. There was nothing in his words that should or could have triggered even a moment of guilt. And yet, Bex felt really guilty.

"Sasha—"

"Yes?"

"Do you—are you—are you, you know, are you okay?" Now what the hell did that mean? Even Bex didn't know what she was trying to say, much less what she'd actually said.

"I am fine," he asserted. "I will to see you tomorrow. Good night, Bex."

"Good night, Sasha."

Bex took a cab to the Bolshoi Theater. As they rounded a corner, she saw Sasha standing at a bus stop. He was leaning against a lamppost, inhaling a cigarette, blowing out a combination of smoke and cold air, and smiling. Bex told herself there was nothing to feel guilty about. He was obviously fine. She had obviously imagined the wistful tone in his voice when she'd told him to go home. He probably had a whole evening planned, telling his girlfriend all about how crazy those Americans were to work for, and also how stupid Bex was, running around, first inside the arena, then outside, then at the hospital, like a chicken with its head cut off (Bex assumed Russian chickens also experienced such life after death), and not coming up with a single, useful piece of information to help her get to the bottom of Igor's murder. Bex imagined the girlfriend laughing and throwing her long, naturally blond, lustrous hair over her shoulder, while looking all worldly-wise and . . . uhm . . . European. Well, Bex could have had long, blond, lustrous hair, too. If she were actually blond. And didn't get all her personal grooming products from a little wicker basket next to the hotel sinks.

In any case, Bex totally had more important things to do with her time than dwell on her hair. As soon as her cab pulled up in front of the Bolshoi Theater, Bex leapt out and, barely taking any time to admire the soaring, multi-column architecture (hadn't Gary Gold told her you don't get to know a country through its architecture?), waved her 24/7 ID badge at the ticket-taker.

The ticket-taker was not impressed.

This actually surprised Bex for a moment. Having spent the last several months of her life exclusively inside locations where a 24/7 ID badge was the equivalent of a free pass anywhere, she had forgotten that there were actually places where—how to put this?—no one cared that she worked for TV.

Luckily, her working for TV had taught Bex that, in the

end, everybody cared about who was paying the bills. And that, if you were connected to anyone paying the bills in any way, you too could pretty much have a free pass to anywhere. So, when the ticket-taker unleashed a barrage of Russian at her, Bex responded with what she gambled might prove the magic word.

"Shell," she said. "Shell Oil."

And then, as the pièce-de-résistance, she pulled out of her parka pocket an old gasoline receipt, with its logo prominently printed on the front, from a Shell Oil station back in the states.

Thank goodness Bex had a tendency to stuff all receipts into her pockets in the hope that something might prove tax-deductible some day. And thank goodness that, prior to heading out on her latest recovery mission, Bex had checked out the Bolshoi Theater's website and learned that their newest sponsor for the 229th season was none other than Shell Oil.

"Oh!" The ticket-taker's eyebrows shot up and she nodded her head fervently, a phony smile replacing the more sincere frown of a moment before. "Shell Oil!" And she stepped aside to let Bex enter.

Another piece of research Bex had completed prior to arrival was to check with the 24/7 business office and find out where the seats that they'd purchased for Lian and her mother were located. Turned out the tickets were for a private box, since that would make it easier to shoot Lian soaking in Russian culture.

Bex ascended the richly carpeted stairs to the mezzanine level, feeling woefully under-dressed. All around her were floor-length gowns, shoulder-length earrings, and cleavage-depth tops. The women wore their hair swept up atop their heads and carried tiny beaded purses with protruding opera glasses, while their men stood by their sides and balanced both their own coats and the requisite minks over one arm, waiting for the coat check to open. The air was so fragrant with flowery perfume and musk perfume and zesty perfume that, by the time Bex got to the top of the stairs, she felt dangerously close to passing out, Dorothy-among-the-Wicked-Witch's-Poppies style.

Bex pushed open the door to Lian's box and nearly tripped over the cameraman's tripod planted squarely at the entrance.

"Hey, Bex," he waved. His soundman, squatting on the floor between the seats so as to stay out of frame, did the same. Amanda and Lian, both sitting in the front row and looking down from the mezzanine into the orchestra seats below, turned their heads in unison. Amanda was wearing a long black skirt and a dark blue blouse buttoned up to the neck. Lian, by contrast, was in pale pink silk, her skirt cut above the knee, her top scooped rather daringly low along the bustline, and covered with a row of matching lace. It was an outfit calculated to make her look like a sophisticated seventeen-year-old, but with no existing bust to back up the tease of the scooped neck, it actually had the opposite effect. She looked like Raggedy Ann stealing Barbie's wardrobe.

"Hi!" Bex said brightly, still winded from her dash up the perfumed steps. And then she asked the cameraman, "Have you shot Lian's singles, yet?"

"No," he said confidently, as if Bex's question made any production sense at all. Fortunately, the unwritten rule at 24/7 was: If your colleague is acting strangely, there is probably a reason, and it probably has to do with the good of the show, so just play along until you figure it out. Had there been no such rule in place, Gil would never be listened to. Bex had been counting on this solidarity from the crew when she snuck in.

"Then I think you should, right away, before the ballet actually starts," Bex said. She turned to Amanda, "Would you mind stepping outside for a moment? We want to get some really nice, close-up shots of Lian that we can use for cutaways and interstitials, and we need the area as clear as possible so that we can match room-tone later."

She'd used a great deal of technical terms, gambling that Amanda wouldn't know what they meant, much less that they shouldn't be together in one sentence. To translate what Bex said in medical terms, she'd basically asked Amanda to hand her a stethoscope so they could perform brain surgery on an X ray, i.e., real technical terms, but gibberish in meaning.

"Oh, yes, of course," Amanda said, "I understand completely," and she tiptoed out of the box. So as not to disturb the . . . uh . . . room-tone.

The camera and soundman looked at Bex expectantly, eager for their next clue. Bex mouthed a silent, "Thanks, guys," and gestured that they could go back to what they were doing. She stepped over the video monitor perched by the camera and plopped into the plush purple seat next to Lian. The upholstery felt like pussy willows and meowed a little when she leaned against it.

"Got a quick question for you, Lian."

"Uh-huh . . ." Lian didn't turn her head and continued watching the milling people below. Bex supposed it might have been a while since Lian found herself a member of an audience, rather than the one in the spotlight.

"It's about the spinning lessons you took from Igor Marchenko."

"The what?" Lian pivoted in her seat, one hand clutching the golden balcony rail to keep from falling into the orchestra. "I didn't take any lessons from Igor. Why should I do that? My spins are good. I get enough revolutions for full credit."

"Well, I don't know about that," Bex lied. As a matter-of-fact, she knew perfectly well that most judges thought Lian's spins were too slow and didn't offer enough changes of position and they would have dearly loved for her to get some extra coaching. "But your mom told me—"

"Mom!" Lian popped out of her seat and, nimbly leaping over the various camera wires scattered about the floor, flung open the door.

Amanda was leaning against the opposite wall, hands behind her back, meeting the curious Russians' furtive glances at the obvious stranger in their midst with an unabashed, all-American "What are you looking at?" stare back.

"Mom!" Lian yelped. "Bex said you told her I went to Igor for spin lessons. That's so stupid. Why would I do that? My spins are fine. And besides, Gary would like, kill me, if I did that."

Amanda's bravado dissipated like a 6.0 after a fall. She glanced from Lian to Bex and back again. She blinked furiously. She didn't say a word.

"Mom!" Lian barked. "What is she talking about? Why would you say that? I never took any lessons from Igor!"

"Amanda . . ." Bex prompted politely, hoping if she actually made her words sound like a question, an answer might be forthcoming.

"What made you think I took lessons from Igor?" Lian ignored her mother and verbally clung to Bex like chewing gum tangled in a ponytail.

Bex looked at Amanda. Lian's doting mother was still apparently pleading the fifth. Unless you counted hyperventilating. Bex figured she had nothing to lose by telling Lian, "I found a check in Igor Marchenko's room. It was made out to him and signed by your mother. When I asked her what it was for, she told me Igor had been secretly giving you spin lessons, without Gary knowing."

"No way," Lian said. "Totally not true. Why would you tell her that, Mom?"

"Because." The hyperventilation made every word Amanda said sound like she was trying to desperately suck it back inside the minute it was uttered. "Because, I had to tell her something."

"Truth is always good," Bex offered, still polite, though suspecting she was about to get over it.

"I couldn't tell you the truth," Amanda puffed.

"Why not?"

"Because." Inside the theater, the Bolshoi orchestra launched into the first, plaintive notes of *Giselle*. The lyrical passage provided an unexpectedly dramatic background to Amanda's confession. "Because, that check I wrote to Igor, it was a bribe. To make sure that Jordan lost Nationals."

Eight

Bex asked, "You were paying Igor to make Jordan lose Nationals? How was that supposed to work? What was he supposed to tell her? *No, Jordan, don't land that jump on one foot, land it on your butt, the judges like it better that way?*"

While being clever, Bex also snuck a side peek at Lian, gauging her reaction to Mommy's confession. She figured if Lian were in on this alleged plot, she would have also known to bluff to Bex about the money being for extra coaching—rather than for a bribe to get the competition to take a dive. The fact that she pretended not to know what Amanda was talking about suggested that Lian was ipso facto pleading innocence to the bribery plot. Unless, that was exactly what Bex was supposed to think.

"You paid Igor to make Jordan lose to me?" Lian asked her mother.

Amanda nodded. Then she shook her head.

"This isn't multiple choice," Bex pointed out.

Amanda wrung her hands. She really did. Bex had read
about panicky people doing so, but she'd never actually seen
the cliché in action. She'd always assumed the expression
came from days gone by, when people still did their wash in
a tub full of soapy water, and that "wringing" your hands re-
ferred to mimicking the action of drying clothes, i.e., turning them this way and that, to get the water out. However, in
this dawn of the twenty-first century, Amanda was making a
more modern, laundry-related gesture. Instead of wringing
the clothes by hand, her nervousness expressed itself in
jerky, jittery fingers. As if she were throwing coins into a
dryer. Did that still count?

"I didn't pay Igor to coach Jordan badly. No. That would
have been silly. No. What I did was . . . the money . . . it was
for Igor to give to Jordan. So that she would skate badly on
purpose. So Lian could win Nationals."

Lian, who, to be fair, did seem to grow more and more
surprised as the story went on, bounced lightly on the tips of
her toes (in synch to the ballet music outside) and asked her
mother, "You mean you didn't think I could win Nationals
on my own, Mommy?"

Amanda stopped tossing imaginary coins into the dryer
and proceeded to unload equally imaginary clothes from the
machine. Her hands bobbed from side to side. "I—I just
wanted you to be happy, Lian. I wanted to help you."

Bex winced, wondering if it would be better to pop back
inside the opera box or simply duck to escape the inevitable
tantrum Amanda had just triggered in her daughter. Because,
in all of Bex's experience interviewing elite athletes, she'd
yet to meet a single one who could face the implication that
they were not capable of winning an event solely on the
basis of their own obviously superior talent, with anything
resembling grace. Or a solid grasp on reality.

Lian's mouth dropped open as she pondered what her
mother had just confessed. And what the confession meant
about Mommy's belief in Lian's ultimate potential. She took

a step forward, raising her arms. Bex wondered if she might actually see some fists flying. And whether it was her responsibility, as the only 24/7 representative on hand to witness the fracas, to interfere before Lian did irrevocable damage to her mother's face. Or, even worse, her sweet little skater reputation. It would be tricky to sell "U.S. vs. Russia: A Figure Skating Challenge" as a battle between good (U.S.) vs. evil (Russia), if one of the good was known to smack her mother around. Especially if you could see the marks.

Gil would be really, really mad if you could see the marks.

"Mommy!" Lian threw her arms around her mother's neck. Was this going to be strangulation, then? "Oh, thank you, thank you, Mommy!"

Ɬℰ𝒳 left the love-fest after several minutes of: "You're the greatest Mommy in the world," and "I would do anything for you, baby. I want what's best for you always, always."

She took a taxi back to the hotel and fell into bed without even checking why the message light was blinking on her phone. She figured she had tomorrow to deal with any crises that might have sprung up during her latest out-of-arena investigation.

When she woke up, the message light was still blinking. How interesting that it never just answered itself.

Bex rubbed her eyes, scratched her arm and, yawning, dialed the retrieval number.

"Hello? Bex? It is Sasha."

She was awake now. She even stopped rubbing and scratching.

"I am calling to say thank you to you. Yesterday, I am learning much about the business of the television. You are being very nice explaining everything to me. Please to have good dreams. I will to see you tomorrow at the production meeting, Bex."

Oh, damn! The production meeting!

Bex ran.

She didn't stop running until she reached the hotel conference room. (And no, technically, she didn't even stop running to pull off the T-shirt she'd slept in and to stumble into her work clothes, including panty hose, long underwear, turtleneck sweater, vest, jeans, parka, thermal socks, and boots; she had actually been heading towards the door the entire time she was getting dressed.) Everyone stared at her as she came in late. But only Sasha smiled.

Bex couldn't help it. She smiled back. He had that effect on people.

Gil asked, "Did we disturb your beauty rest, Bex?"

She stopped smiling. She couldn't help it. Gil had that effect on people, too.

"Sorry," Bex mumbled. Then, realizing that every seat around the conference table was already taken, she went to slump against the wall.

This seemed to make Gil happy.

"Bex," he said. "We were just talking about you."

Great.

"We're cutting together this piece on Marchenko buying the bucket for the first half of the broadcast, and we've got a problem."

Oh, no. Here it came. Bex felt certain Gil was about to publicly harangue her for not knowing who the killer was, thus leaving his piece without a "button." She got ready to blush, squirm, and otherwise wonder why she thought this was such a terrific job in the first place.

"We've got no footage of Marchenko's family," Gil made a circle in the air with his pen, indicating a great, big zero. "Zip from when he competed for Russia, definitely zip from his America days, and zip this time around. What I'm thinking we need to do, we need to track down his family and get their take on the whole poison-a-roo."

"That's a great idea, Gil," Bex said, somewhat in awe. Not only because Gil had come up with a great idea but, because, for a change, Bex actually concurred that it was a great idea. Even if she had thought of it, first, yesterday. "I'll get right on it," Bex said.

She wasn't one to let a tiny thing like not knowing how exactly she was going to do that dampen her enthusiasm.

Ĥℰℛ first stop was the Moscow phone book. There were fifty-seven Marchenkos listed. Bex decided, on first pass, to skip the men's names, since she knew Igor's mother had been single at the time of his defection and, if she'd married in the interim, she'd have a different name, anyway. (Bex really hoped she hadn't married in the interim.)

The exclusion narrowed the possibilities down to thirty-three. Bex let Sasha man the phones, which he did with his usual good humor. He endured six no-answers; eleven angry, "No one here by that name, you fool! Why don't you go stick your head a) under a train, b) in a toilet, c) . . . "—Sasha wouldn't translate out of respect for Bex's modest ears;" and six old people thrilled for the chance to speak to anyone at all. Then, still talking, he finally gestured enthusiastically at the receiver with his index finger, mouthing, "Yes!"

From the vehement sounds on the other end, the prospect of being invaded by an American television crew did not appear thrilling to Igor's mother and/or sister.

Bex listened to Sasha cajoling. Followed by more audio negativity. Followed by pleading. Followed by a little less negativity. Followed by a plethora of charm. A smile. A joke. He even seemed to be winking over the phone.

Followed by a sigh. A *dosvedanya*. And Sasha telling Bex, "Let us go."

• • •

The cab ride took forty-five minutes. After the first fifteen, they left behind the relative color and joy of downtown Moscow and entered an area two shades grayer than Bex would have previously thought possible. On either side of them loomed towering, nondescript apartment buildings, their top floors obscured by sloppily dripping clouds, their entryways by sad, shivering trees. Periodically, they'd see an old man dressed in a floor-length coat and sheep-fur hat come out of one of the buildings, stomp his feet, and frown at the world before trudging off. Or a woman of indeterminate age dragging a child wrapped up under a knit hat with a kerchief over his ears and a loose pom-pom on top. The child might, in turn, be dragging a sled. But mostly, it was just apartment buildings, identically grim streets, and a smattering of cars with at least one rusty sector.

Bex thought of the hospital they'd visited earlier and asked Sasha, "I take it this is one of the best neighborhoods in Moscow?"

"Oh, no," he looked at her in surprise. "The people who live here, in the days of communism, they must to do something wrong. Is a punishment."

"What about now?"

"Now," he shrugged. "Maybe it is habit."

"Or home," Bex offered.

"Yes." As soon as Sasha repeated the word, Bex realized it wasn't one he could be too familiar with. "Home."

That's good, Bex, she sighed to herself. *Remind an orphan about home. What are you going to do next? Refuse him a second bowl of gruel?*

The latter, at least, turned out not to be a problem.

Despite what, to Bex, had sounded like a distinctive lack of enthusiasm for their visit over the phone, Igor Marchenko's mother, Luba, and his sister, Svetlana, had nonetheless loaded up their dining room table with food in anticipation of their arrival. Just by peeking around the corner, Bex spied a platter of sandwiches. Black rye bread, butter, and equally black caviar. A blue ceramic bowl held sweetly browned pierogi, overstuffed with cabbage. Sliced sugared jellies were arranged like a rainbow on top of a clear glass platter. Four flower-pattern cups, with matching saucers and silver spoons, were set out for tea next to a second glass platter holding creamy meringue stacked like a pyramid.

Luba and Svetlana gestured for Bex and Sasha to please come in, take off their coats, have a seat, drink some tea, have some food. But first, the Marchenkos had to shoo away their staring neighbors. Though, maybe, *neighbors* wasn't the right word. To Bex, neighbors were people who lived across the street from you, or in the house next door to you, or, at the very closest, in an apartment that shared a wall with yours. But these people—an elderly woman, her look-alike (except for a mustache) son, his sour-faced wife, and caterwauling, bare-bottomed toddler twins, a boy and a girl—actually lived right inside of Svetlana and Luba's apartment. It was called a communal, a holdover from a time when the Soviet government had assigned two or more completely unrelated families to share what had once been a single-clan dwelling. Igor's mother and sister resided in the former living room. The other family owned the two smaller bedrooms in the back—one for the married couple, one for Grandma and the twins. All seven people shared a single kitchen and bathroom.

And they also, apparently, shared a keen interest in each other's private business, as indicated by the fact that, as soon as Bex and Sasha walked in, Grandma and her nosy kin magically materialized from inside their own rooms to unabashedly stare at them.

Bex may not have understood Russian all that well, but she certainly got the gist of Luba's waving the entire brood away, yelling for them to mind their own business and stay out of her way. She also had a pretty good idea as to what guttural words the man-of-the-house spewed in return.

After the vitriol-filled exchange however, the other family did retreat, grumbling, to their own area, leaving Bex and Sasha alone with Igor's mother and sister.

According to Bex's research, Luba Marchenko was about seventy years old. Her daughter, Svetlana—"Sveta" was the preferred diminutive, Bex knew—was forty-eight; six years older than her brother. Having pondered newspaper photos of young Igor at the time of his defection, Bex could definitely see the resemblance between his adolescent features and the women of his family. All three shared blue eyes surrounded by nearly white lashes, full Slavic lips, and high cheekbones. Svetlana's hair was still the corn-silk blond that Igor's had been. She wore it very short, and the ends brushed her ears like Igor's had. Their mother's hair was completely gray now, worn in a long braid that she wound atop her head and fastened with pins.

Bex tried to thank them both for allowing her to come and ask some questions. She used the few Russian words— *spacibo*, *horosho*—that she actually did know.

But Svetlana interrupted to say, "We speak English. My mother a little bit, and me, more. I studied English at the school."

"Eat, eat." Igor's mother urged Bex to partake of a caviar sandwich even before she'd had a chance to sit down. And, while salted fish eggs were not usually her idea of an appetizing breakfast, Bex dove right in. A mouth full of bread, butter, and caviar gave her a chance to look around before feeling compelled to ask questions.

Back home in New York City, Bex lived in a studio apartment. A rather small studio apartment, even by NYC standards. Bex owned three pieces of furniture. A foldout sofa bed, a desk, and a stand for her TV. She had the desk and the TV-stand against one wall, and the sofa bed against another.

When she unfolded the sofa bed, its metallic frame scraped against the front of the desk, its sides pressed against the walls. Like Bex said, it was a very small apartment.

And she had a lot of stuff. Books, CDs, magazines, clothes, pictures, souvenir knick-knacks from her travels, flyers touting local events she wanted to check out but probably wouldn't because of her travels. Which was why Bex was always complaining that she didn't have enough space for the stuff she'd accumulated. But Bex was twenty-four years old, and she'd only lived in her studio for a year. Luba and Svetlana were two people who'd shared their one room for almost thirty years. And still, the place was neater than Bex's domicile.

Each of the twin beds on either wall was covered by a freshly ironed bedspread. Their glass and wood china cabinet may have been stuffed with dishes, crystal vases, and ceramic figurines of rosy-cheeked animals from Russian folktales, but there wasn't a spec of dust in sight. Thick rugs hung from three of the walls to keep the cold out. The fourth wall, though, the one directly across from the door so that it was the first thing you saw upon entering, was the Igor Marchenko Memorial Wall.

It wasn't titled as such, naturally, but Bex wondered what else you would call a wall that, first and foremost, boasted a legal-paper–sized black-and-white portrait of Igor at the age of eight or so, dressed in a homemade skating outfit with a large V at the chest, performing a stag jump, arms crossed, one leg stretched out, the other tucked under him? Beneath that picture was a series of smaller photos, Igor-through-the-ages, each showing him on the ice or with a trophy in his hands. The actual trophies jostled for space upon a little wooden perch underneath the gallery. They, too, were devoid of any dust.

Bex pulled a digital camera out of her pocket, and asked, "Can I take a picture?"

Gil would have her head for not bringing a camera crew

to document the scene—it was just the kind of heart-jerker he believed fans were watching 24/7 for—but maybe this would make up for it.

"No!" Luba and Svetlana both protested much more vehemently than Bex might have expected. Svetlana even jumped in front of the display, to block Bex's shot.

"Why not?" Bex asked, genuinely confused. This shrine had obviously been built to honor Igor. Why wouldn't they want it seen?

"No television," Svetlana insisted. "Not inside our home. He cannot know you were here. He told us, we must not talk to anyone about Igor, or there will be danger!"

Nine

"Who?" Bex only managed to get out a single, English word. In that time, Sasha had already leapt in with a flurry of Russian, triggering another flurry of responses from Svetlana and Luba.

Completely lost on the speech side, Bex tried to guess what was going on from their body language. Both Svetlana and Luba were shaking their heads, waving their arms, pointing out the window, down the street, to the phone, to Bex, to the pictures of Igor, to Sasha, then shaking their heads some more and practically wailing. Sasha continued asking calm, measured questions, never raising his voice or allowing himself to be derailed. At least, that's what Bex hoped he was doing. All she knew was that he was the only one in the room not shouting.

Well, except for Bex. Who was simply standing there, mute, watching the fracas as if it were a tennis match.

After several minutes—during which time the twins' mother poked her head in and presumably screamed for them all to be quiet, prompting Luba to take a break from yelling at Sasha to howl back at the mother until she grabbed her kids and disappeared—Sasha managed to calm both women down to the point where they stopped yelling. They sat down, Luba on her bed, Svetlana on a chair closest to the dining table. They were still trying to explain something to Sasha, but the shrieks had deflated into yelps.

"Tell Bex," Sasha ordered in English. He rested his hands on Bex's shoulders and guided her until she stood directly in Luba and Svetlana's sightline. Bex wondered if she should maybe be doing something to encourage the process, yet nothing useful came immediately to mind.

"Tell Bex, please, what you have told me," Sasha repeated.

Luba and Svetlana looked at each other across the small room, both took a deep breath in preparation, then closed their mouths without saying a word. Each seemed to be willing the other to go first. Bex decided to speed up the process by offering, "You know, I never got a chance to offer my condolences about Igor's death. I'm really sorry. I know you must have missed him so much all these years he was gone. Did you at least get a chance to see him before . . . before?"

Luba shook her head. She covered her face with her hands, pressing both palms hard against her cheekbones as if squeezing back tears, but, when she lowered her arms, her eyes were dry. She shook her head again.

Svetlana said, "No. We did not. We could not."

"Why?"

Mother and daughter exchanged glances again. Luba seemed content to let Sveta speak for both of them, so her daughter damned the Kalishnikovs and plunged ahead. She said, "We were frightened. The man who called, he warned us not to come and see Igor, or there would be danger."

"I don't understand. Someone threatened you? Who was it?"

Sasha suggested, "Maybe you should explain to her from

the beginning. So she understands. This is difficult for her to understand. She is American."

Bex wondered what that was supposed to mean. Yet the epithet(?), compliment(?), fact(?), appeared to make perfect sense to Luba and Svetlana.

Igor's sister nodded. She looked over her shoulder at the picture of Igor as a little boy, and began: "Igor was selected for joining number one skating group at Moscow rink when he is ten years old. It is the big honor. Important coaches believe Igor is talented, he can be champion for U.S.S.R. It is the big honor, and the big fortune for us, his family. When Igor win Junior World Championship one year later, we are given apartment of our own to live in. Not communal. A bedroom for Igor, Mama sleeps in the front room, and a bedroom for me and my husband, Fedor. It is like dream, having so much space. We are very happy."

Bex was about to say that she could imagine. And then she realized that no, she actually couldn't in the slightest.

"When Igor defects," Sveta continued, "we lose everything. Not only apartment. My husband and I, we lose our places in the University. Fedor was studying to be doctor, I to be an engineer. We are called in front of our classes, and the Komsomol leader—that is the leader of the young Communist Party group, she stands us in front of our class and she calls us many awful names. We are traitors to our motherland, we are criminals. We spit on everything the U.S.S.R. gave us as gifts, she says. And then our fellow students, they stand up, one by one by one. My best friend, she is girl I study with since the first form in school, she tells everyone I have always been traitor, that I would rip pictures of Lenin out of our schoolbooks, that I talk about rnnning away to America and going on American television and telling lies about the Soviet Union. That I never come to the required May Day parades. I came to every parade! And I wore my young pioneer uniform proudly! I never . . ." Svetlana trailed off.

She took a moment to collect herself. And then she went on. "It does not matter now. Because soon Fedor leaves me. He tells me Igor and my family ruined his future. His whole life. He goes to medical school in Siberia. He thinks maybe the disgrace is not so severe there, and they will let him finish his education. But I cannot do this. I cannot leave Mama. I am all she has left."

At that, Luba reached over to squeeze her daughter's hand. "Sveta is very good girl," she said softly.

Svetlana gestured around the room they were standing in. "Mama and I are sent here to live. Communal, again. It is not the most awful. It is used to it and, I think, we can adjust, we can survive. We are strong. But, then . . ."

"Yes?" Bex prompted. "What happened then?"

"Then the others come."

"What others? You mean your neighbors? The other family?"

It took Sveta a moment to understand what Bex was asking and, when she finally did, she simply laughed. "Oh, no. No, no, no, no . . . The other family, they are here before we arrive. Not the woman and the two children, but the old woman and her son and her husband, then. No, they do not bother us. Not more than average. It is life, we do not complain. No, who comes a few months after us, it is that man, Valeri Konstantin, the team leader of Igor's group. And Igor's coach, Alexandr Troika. They are both judged to be punished, like us, for Igor's defection. They also to lose their apartments. They also sent here. Only difference is, they have much nicer apartments before. We—we are used to live like this. Not Konstantin. Not Troika. And especially not Troika's wife. The first day they are sent here, Konstantin and Troika, they are both drunk, they come to stand under our window and they throw rocks! They break the glass! They are calling us the most awful, horrible names. Names you should never say in front of woman. They yell so loudly, one neighbor of ours, she pours boiling water on them from teakettle to make them go away. But this does not stop them. For many years later, they come back. Troika, he grabs me in the hallway of my home, and he presses me against the wall. He hits my head and he threatens to . . . he threatens . . . he is an evil man, I think. He tells me his wife, she is so angry with him about he and she living here, that she will not . . . he says if she will not, then I should . . . he says . . ." This time, Svetlana seemed sincerely out of words. She bit her lip and stared out the window.

Her mother picked up the story. She told Sasha something in Russian and urged him to translate for Bex.

Sasha cleared his throat. "She says this abuse of them, it went on for many years. Particularly awful after Igor won the Olympics. Do you know, after the scores went up and Igor was declared the winner, the entire television network in all of Russia went to a black screen, and then, a few moments later, they began showing the skiing event. Igor's name was never mentioned again during the games. Except by Konstantin. The night Igor won, he smeared dog excrement all over their door and the walls. The neighbors, all of them on this floor, they made Luba and Sveta clean it up, wipe it up with their hands and their skirts and . . . and their mouths. They drag them out of their apartment by the hair and they threw them on the ground and they pour buckets of dirty water over them, yelling for them to clean it up, clean it up, you traitors, you criminals."

Bex thought she might be sick. But, strangely, she seemed to be the only one. In Svetlana and Luba's cases, Bex could guess it was because this all happened so long ago, they'd had time to make peace with it. Or at least, they had lost the capacity to be hurt by it. Sasha, on the other hand, as he relayed the story, seemed utterly nonplussed by the tale. He wasn't unemotional. He seemed authentically sympathetic to what the women had gone through, if Bex could judge by the gentle way he'd questioned them, and the calm manner in which he translated Luba's words. But he also didn't appear shocked by anything he was saying. In fact, his tone sounded more resigned than anything else. As if he'd expected no different and was simply doing his duty by educating Bex about how this part of the world, his part of the world, worked.

Bex felt genuinely sorry for what Luba and Sveta had gone through. But she was most upset by how Sasha seemed to accept their treatment as a matter of course.

"Did you do anything about this?" Bex demanded. She could hear how harsh her voice sounded and she realized that it was inappropriate. But, the reality was, their tale, in combination with their passivity in telling it, had made her angry. She knew she had no right to be angry, especially not at the victims. And yet she was. "Did you contact the police? Did you complain? What did you do about the way you were treated?"

To Bex's disappointment, if not exactly to her surprise, all three acted as resigned to her unwarranted cross-examination as they had to the initial violence.

Luba spread her hands helplessly. Svetlana simply shook her head. And it was Sasha who explained, "There is no one who could help them. What Igor did, it was the worst of worse crimes in the Soviet Union. They are very lucky they were not sent out of the city, or put in prison or . . ."

"We were very lucky," Sveta agreed.

"How long did Konstantin and Troika go on harassing you?" Bex asked.

"Oh, not long, not long," Sveta reassured. "When the Soviet Union is over, and the past is forgotten, Konstantin, he receives place back in skating federation. He is very happy. He leaves us alone, thank the God."

Bex crunched some quick numbers. Igor defected in 1977. The Soviet Union officially collapsed in 1991. Even assuming Konstantin was reinstated the moment Boris Yeltsin climbed atop that tank, that still left fourteen years for the Marchenkos to suffer.

Not long, Svetlana had said. *Not long at all.*

"What about Alexandr Troika? I know he wasn't reinstated. Konstantin told me it was too late, no one remembered him, no one wanted to train with him, anymore."

Luba said something to Sasha. Sasha translated, "That is true. He did not return to coaching."

"So what happened to him?"

Sveta said, "Nothing happened to him. He lives, he works. Sometimes, when he drinks very much, he still comes to scream at us. But now it is different. In the past, when someone comes to scream about traitors to Mother Russia, the neighbors, they do not dare to stop him, or some other neighbor maybe report them to police as supporting non-loyal activity. But now, when he comes to yell, the neighbors, they are not afraid of being called traitors, too, so they yell for him to shut his mouth and they force him to go away. This goes on for a while, and he stops yelling. Maybe years have passed since he comes to bother us. He is just old, angry man now. I see his wife on the street, she does not talk to me. She gives me the evil eye and she spits, but she does not talk. So it is over, I think. Everyone has forgotten."

"But, you said someone called you. Before Igor came back to Russia, you said someone called you and warned you not to see him, or there would be danger."

"Konstantin." Luba finally spoke up without using Sasha as a go-between. Her eyes radiating anger for the first time since Bex came in, she spat out, "Konstantin."

"Valeri Konstantin called you?" Bex felt she needed to clarify. "The president of the Russian Figure Skating Federation called and threatened you?"

"Yes," Sveta said. "He phone us himself. The week before Igor was coming. He tell us not to come to arena for competition. He remind us, he knows where we live. He knows where Mama work, and where I work. He say there will be great danger to us if we come to see Igor."

"Did he say why he didn't want you to come?"

"It is because, if Mama and I come to arena, there will be newspaper writers there, and he think they will ask us many questions about Igor's defection. Konstantin is afraid we will tell the world what he do to us many years ago. He is president of federation. It will sound very bad for him."

Bex agreed. It would sound very bad for him. In fact, it was exactly the kind of messy scandal a man could lose his cushy federation position over, especially if the International Skating Union (ISU), concerned about their own image by association, put pressure on him to step down. Bex imagined that, if the details got out, Konstantin could find himself back exactly where Igor Marchenko's defection first put him—which was nowhere in skating, with no hope even, this time around, for a regime-change reprieve.

Bex knew it was petty and childish but, at that moment, she very much wanted the story to get out. And she, even more, wanted to be the one in charge of dispersing it.

She asked Sveta and Luba, "Did you even get the chance to see Igor again before he died? Did he maybe stop by here . . ."

Luba shook her head.

Sveta explained, "After the competition, Igor said. He said, let me to finish my work, so I am free, then I will come to see you. And then, he said, I will come home."

Bex and Sasha took the stairs down from the eleventh floor. There was, in theory, an elevator, which they had ridden up an hour earlier. But, after waiting ten minutes and not seeing the overhead numbers so much as budge, they decided to give up false hope and trek on down. The stairway was illuminated by a single uncovered fluorescent light bulb dangling from the ceiling. Which seemed to be smashed and even the chain stolen on every floor divisible by three. Bex and Sasha kept their hands on the sticky railing (good thing it was winter and gloves were handy, though Bex planned to ditch hers in the nearest garbage can as soon as they stepped outside), and followed the reeking aroma of human urine, which grew stronger the closer they got to the ground.

Bex and Sasha had barely set foot in the lobby when they were accosted. It was Sveta and Luba's mustached neighbor, and he obviously wanted to make some point very, very clear.

Despite Bex's lack of Russian fluency, even she could recognize the same few words repeated over and over again.

Sasha said, "This is Vadim. He would like you to know something."

"I'm listening," Bex said.

"He would like you to know that his neighbors, the women, they are big liars, and you must not believe their lies."

"I see . . ." Bex smiled politely at Vadim, who was watching her intently and nodding along with Sasha's translation, though he presumably didn't understand a word that was being said. "Does he have any proof of his assertions?"

Sasha relayed Bex's query. Russian followed.

"He says you can ask anyone in the building. They will tell you. The women are liars. They want Americans to believe all Russians are savages. They are not savages. They are good people. His father was a veteran of the Great Patriotic War."

That was nice. If irrelevant. Though Vadim's local character reference did give Bex an idea. She prompted Sasha. "Could you ask Vadim, please, if he recalls where exactly around here Alexandr Troika still lives?"

It turned out that Igor's former coach and Konstantin's alleged partner in crime was located in an identical high-rise two blocks away. On the fourteenth floor this time. And with an elevator that didn't even pretend to be working. The door was open when Bex and Sasha got there. It had apparently been turned into a makeshift trash receptacle several days—

or weeks—before. Bex would have thrown her soiled gloves into the pile of old liquor bottles, rotting food, and torn-up mail, except that she still had another dim stairwell to conquer, and she wasn't counting on this one being any more hygienic.

"We're getting quite a workout, aren't we?" Bex huffed as she and Sasha puffed up the stairs. "Both mind and body. I mean, these stair marathons are a pain, but I think my brain actually hurts more from trying to figure out who's lying and who's telling the truth, and who's only telling a half-life, and who's—"

"The truth." Sasha stopped suddenly, turning around so that he and Bex only had a step between them. In the dim light, his question sounded even more sinister than he'd probably meant it. Probably. "Why does the truth matter?"

Well, that certainly stopped Bex in her proverbial tracks. "What do you mean? Why do you think we're doing all this? We're trying to figure out who killed Igor."

"Yes. I understand this. But why does the truth matter?"

What had Winston Churchill said about America and England being two countries divided by a common language? Bex was definitely feeling very Great Britain-y right now. She stammered, "How are we going to know the truth, if we don't get the truth?"

"But, Russian people," Sasha spoke hesitantly, also apparently struggling with something lost in translation, "they do not know the truth."

"You mean, like, if they tripped over it?"

Sasha stared at her blankly. Bex made a stern mental note: Keep the American idioms to a minimum. The guy was having a tough enough time as it was.

Sasha said, "It is hard to explain."

"I'm listening," Bex prompted. And she was, too. Note the utter lack of sarcasm that had been going on for seconds now. She really did want to try and understand what he was attempting to explain to her.

"Before," Sasha said, "with the Communists, the truth, it changed all the time. One day, America is Russia's ally in World War II, the next day, it is the enemy and all contact is forbidden. My father, he tells me this anecdote about his father. His father was teacher of geology. One day, he shows to his class, look what a colleague from the city of Sydney, Australia, send me. It is a piece of old rock . . . I do not know the English word for this." Sasha apologized, then went on, "My grandfather says to his class: let us study this old rock and explore how it is different from old Russian rock. The next day, my grandfather is arrested for contact with the West. He dies in prison. Because he did not know rules changed about what is good and what is bad."

"That's awful," Bex said, hearing how glib she sounded, but eager to skip over the unpleasantness to her question. "But what does that have to do with finding out the truth? Your grandfather told the truth. He just got punished for it."

"Yes. And because many people like my grandfather suffered because they said what is truthfully on their mind, Russian people, they learn that what is on your mind, it should have no relation to what you say. To save yourself, you must always, always say what the person who is asking question, wants to hear. What the truth is, this is not important. It is not—what is the word?—*relevant*. Yes, it is not relevant."

"So you're saying that everyone in Russia just lies about everything all the time?" It seemed a rather odd basis on which to rest a culture.

"No, no, no. Not lying. They say what needs to be said, to be safe."

"Have you been doing that all this time, with me?" Bex had no idea where that question came from. It had nothing to do with what they were talking about and, frankly, she couldn't even think of anything Sasha had told her where it would matter that it was a lie. Except that she really needed to know. Had he been putting on an act with her?

"Of course," Sasha said. No guilt, not even a hesitation.

"Oh."

"I am your assistant. My job is to do the things you need your assistant to do. I do what you ask, all the time."

"You mean, whether you want to or not?"

"It does not matter what I want," Sasha continued to explain patiently. "I do what I need to do, to get what I need to get."

"So, you mean you haven't wanted to help me?"

"It is my job," Sasha said. "I want to help you because it is my job."

"So you don't really want to help me?"

She'd lost him. Even in the dim lighting, Bex could tell by the perplexed frown on Sasha's face that she'd lost him. Which was fair enough, since Bex didn't completely understand what he was trying to tell her, either.

She was ready to call the whole thing off, except for one thing. Bex really wanted to know, "So, do you mean you've only been pretending to like me?"

It wasn't a fair question, she got that much. For one thing, Bex had never asked him if he liked her, so there was nothing there for him to lie about. For another thing, liking her was hardly a condition of his employment. (God forbid, if that standard was ever applied to Bex and Gil Cahill.) And for a third thing, why was she asking for an honest answer from a person who'd just told her that, in his culture, there was no such thing? Wasn't she just asking him to lie about lying?

Sasha said, "I do to like you, Bex."

And then he turned around and continued trudging up the stairs.

She wanted to run after him.

In fact, she did just that.

She kind of had to. The last thing Bex needed was to get trapped alone inside this finalist for Smelliest Stairs Ever.

She also wanted to ask him about a million questions about what he had just said. About liking her, that is. All that other profound cultural stuff, that could wait.

But she never got the chance. They were at Alexandr Troika's door before Bex had managed to formulate the exact, perfect query. So what if that formulation happened to have taken her three floors. You couldn't rush perfection.

Sasha took the liberty of knocking. She was grateful for that. Her knocks on the doors of total strangers tended to sound like timid taps, more questions than demands. Sasha knocked as if he expected to be answered, and he expected to be answered now.

So, naturally, he was.

A woman cracked open the door, its ringed, metal chain still cautiously in place. She was in her middle or late forties, Bex guessed based on the one-third of her she could see through the slit. Her hair had recently been dyed presumably in an attempt to go blond. The attempt had failed. She was more green, with a silver tinge. It matched the two capped teeth on either side of her top incisors.

Sasha said something in Russian. Bex could only make out the words Alexandr and Troika.

In response, the woman laughed harshly. It might have been a cough.

She said something long and detailed, to which Sasha replied with another stream of the incomprehensible, out of which Bex plucked the names Valeri Konstantin and Igor Marchenko. Sasha pointed to Bex. She smiled and tried to look worthy.

Her smiles seemed to upset the woman further. Her cough turned into a bark.

A bark and then a slam of the door in Sasha's face.

Had that gone well? Bex couldn't tell.

Sasha said, "She is Alexandr Troika's wife. She says Alexandr is not here. She says he moved away two years ago. She does not know where he is now."

"Did you ask her about what Luba and Svetlana said? About the way Alexandr and Konstantin treated them?"

"Yes. She said those two women—she uses very bad words; I will not say them in English to you—she said they deserve everything bad in the past and in the future, too. Her husband always say that Igor ruin his life. Everything bad that happens to him, it is because Igor is traitor to his country and to his coach. Alexandr tell his wife, if he has chance ever, he will to kill Igor."

Ten

"So, we have our killer." Bex made a big show of rubbing her palms one against the other, indicating visual completion. "Good. Let's go home."

Sasha smiled. Then he stopped. And kind of frowned. Good. Let him wonder if she was telling the truth, for a change.

Bex marveled at her ability to be so bitter over something that had happened so recently. Still, it did give her helpful insight into her multitude of suspects. If Bex could be so cranky over Sasha—what? *confusing* her just a few minutes ago—she could only imagine how cranky Alexandr Troika, Gary Gold, Valeri Konstantin, Luba, and Svetlana Marchenko felt over Igor's virtually destroying their lives thirty years ago.

Sasha said, "You are joking, yes?"

"I don't know." Bex did her petulant child act, disheartened because only she knew exactly how much of an act it was not. "Maybe I'm just not telling the truth."

Sasha smiled.

It was not the response Bex had been hoping for. He was supposed to be crushed and demoralized. Not amused.

Bex waited for him to ask a follow-up question, or at least to challenge her earlier declaration. Bex hoped his questioning her meaning would allow her to casually but with a purpose, reopen their earlier discussion on the stairway. Because she really did want to reopen their earlier discussion on the stairway. Albeit without him knowing just how much she wanted to reopen said discussion.

Bex figured she could lead Sasha where she needed without her being too obvious about it. After all, wasn't this what she did all the time with her interview subjects?

But Sasha wasn't her typical interview subject. He was either much smarter than them or much dumber. Because, despite Bex's best attempts, he either pretended not to understand what she was talking about, or he really didn't understand.

In any case, while she waited for him to step into her carefully baited trap, Sasha turned around, walked to the curb, and hailed a taxi.

They didn't talk much on the way back to the arena. Bex felt like pouting, and Sasha felt like letting her. Or maybe he didn't even know that she was pouting. Ever since his confession (or was it all part of a scheme to "get what I want"?) about the flexibility of honesty in Russia, Bex found herself questioning every word he uttered for double, triple, and quadruple meaning. Which was why his simple query of "What would you like to do next?" managed to keep her busy for the duration of the ride.

It was only when they piled out of the taxi and started walking towards the arena doors that Bex realized she still owed him an answer. There were three days of work left on this show, and she couldn't exactly ignore him the entire time. Especially when, for the life of her, Bex couldn't even put her finger on why she wanted to.

"You know what I need you to do?" Bex asked Sasha, and he sprung to attention like a jack-in-the-box. Only yesterday, Bex had found his enthusiasm endearing. Now she wondered if it was all part of a complex plot to make her believe . . . something. Probably something insidious. "Could you take a walk around the arena and see if you can track down the holistic-medicine guy? He's got to come back to his spot, sometime.

"I can do that," Sasha bobbed his head and took off.

Bex tried to pry satisfaction from knowing that she'd sent him to wander around in the cold Moscow winter, while she stayed inside the arena, safe and warm. It was a strangely unfulfilling victory.

Especially when Bex looked around and realized that, even with the victory, she was still inside a dank gray sports arena, with nothing better to do than continue asking surly, uncooperative people to answer, for the second time, questions they hadn't been so thrilled with on the first go-around.

She figured she might as well start the pointless exercise with Jordan Ares since, at least in her case, Bex did have a few new queries to throw into the mix. No more just, "Where were you the morning your coach was killed?" Bex now had Amanda Reilly's check to ask about, as well as Lian's doting Mommy's claim that the money was for Jordan to take a dive at Nationals. Bex figured it was time to find out what Jordan had to say about the arrangement.

Bex first looked for Jordan at the practice rink, but found only "Russian" girls on the ice. Both of them were skating cautiously, each nursing their respective injuries. And grudges. It made their performances less than exciting to watch. Brittany winced in pain every time she pulled in her arms to spin, prompting her to stop abruptly and flop, dejected, out of it, as if someone had unexpectedly yanked the rip cord. As for Galina, she had been visibly rattled by Brittany's threats to damage her skates. The redheaded whirling dervish didn't trust the stability of her blades, causing her to hesitate just enough on her take-offs and landings to completely eviscerate the timing of her jumps. The girl who won her first major title by executing quadruple rotations, could barely complete a double-jump now without buckling. And, every time she stumbled, Galina would glare at Brittany. Every time Brittany winced, she glared at Galina. Although Bex noticed that, despite the revulsion, both doggedly stuck to their own sides of the practice ice, and that neither one made so much as a move towards approaching, much less engaging the other.

They'd either learned their joint lessons about tussling this close to a televised competition, or something more important: the fear of Valeri Konstantin, which had been drummed into them by none other than the great man, himself

Unlike the other day, when the president of the federation had been content to sit in the stands and watch his skaters from above, he now stood—not even sat—rink-side, arms folded across his chest, eyes tracking the girls' every move. He did not look like a happy federation president. And he most certainly did not look like a man eager to chat with Bex about his past as a taunter of innocent women, and his present as a threatener of same. That, Bex decided, was a discussion that could wait until he looked less ready to commit murder. Possibly for the second time that week.

She called Jordan at her hotel and, upon getting no answer, checked with the production office to see if Jordan was out anywhere with a video crew. She wasn't.

But when Bex asked if anyone knew where she might find Jordan, the same cameraman who'd earlier played along with her scamming Lian and Amanda, now smirked and told Bex cryptically, "Just track the fumes."

Bex didn't know what he meant. Until, following the helpful stretch of the cameraman's finger, she walked a few feet down the arena hall, and saw the smoke wafting from underneath the closed door to one of the ballet rooms. It smelled like a menthol cigarette convention. Bex guessed she'd found her girl.

She tried the knob. It was locked. She knocked.

"Yeah, hold on a second!"

A few minutes of frantic rustling, and then Jordan appeared in the doorway. All signs of cigarettes gone. Except for the smoke that continued wafting out of the garbage can by the open window. An open window. In the middle of winter, in Moscow. Sure. Nothing suspicious about that.

Bex said, "I can still smell them, you know."

"It's none of your business, you know."

"Did Igor let you smoke?"

"None of his business either. Not anymore, for sure."

"Doesn't smoking hurt your skating?"

"Do you want something?"

"Actually, yes." Bex stepped inside the murky room and, with a cough, closed the door behind them. "Let's have some privacy."

"You coming on to me?"

"Amanda Reilly has made a very interesting accusation against you."

"Oh, what now? That I've got a Lian voodoo doll I stick with pins every time darling Lian skates; that's why she can't land her triple-triple?"

"Amanda said she was paying you to deliberately lose next Nationals and default the title to Lian."

A beat. No reaction. No denial, no affirmation, no flip remark. And then Jordan said, "I don't know what Mrs. Reilly's been smoking, but where can I get my hands on some of that good stuff?"

Well, at least Bex had gotten her flip remark, so she knew Jordan was paying attention.

"You're saying it's not true?"

"She got proof, or she just shooting her mouth off, like usual?"

"A check," Bex said. "Igor had a check in his hotel room made out to him from Amanda Reilly. When I asked her what it was for, she told me they'd made a deal to get Lian the National title."

"Let's see it," Jordan said. "The check. Let's see if you're telling the truth."

Unused to being challenged—most people tended to accept her assertions at face value, whether they were true or not—Bex felt a touch offended as she dug around in her research file to produce the rectangular piece of paper.

Jordan stared at the check in Bex's hand. She seemed to be reading each letter and numeral, vetting them for authenticity. And then, in a flash, she snatched it out of Bex's hand, slipping it into the pocket of her jeans before Bex even had the chance to react. (Not that she was sure what she'd have done given the chance to react. Bex didn't relish the idea of wrestling a word-class athlete. Unlike the evenly matched Galina and Brittany knockdown, this would not come even close to being a fair fight.)

"Okay, you caught me," Jordan said. "It's all true."

"What?" Bex had been so busy imagining the literal whiplash she would get from trying to tackle Jordan for the check that she wasn't prepared for the mental episode Jordan's out-of-the-blue confession inspired. "What did you say?"

"I said, you're right. You win. You're the best gosh-darn researcher ever, yadda, yadda, yadda; nothing gets by you."

"And in English?"

"Amanda told you the truth. We had a deal. The three of us. Her cash for my skating like crap at Nationals and letting Lian win."

Bex said, "That doesn't sound like you. I've watched you

all season. You don't give away a fraction of a point if you can help it. You're a hard-core competitor."

"I'm also a realist." Apparently, when Jordan got excited, she forgot to speak like white trash and actually grew articulate. "Skating costs an insane amount of money. I don't have enough. I never have enough. Amanda Reilly, her price was right. And it was only for one competition. Just Nationals. Hell, if her precious Lian wants to win so badly . . . The U.S. can send three girls to Worlds this year, so even if I don't take it all at Nationals, I can still make the World Team. She didn't say I couldn't make the World Team. And a World Title is more important than Nationals in the long run anyway. And it was just for one competition."

"Igor agreed to this?"

"Amanda said he did, didn't she?"

"Do you know if he'd ever done this before, with any of his other students?" If he had, Bex suddenly had a whole new line of inquiry to pursue.

"How should I know?"

"And why is the check made out to him, instead of to you?"

Jordan shrugged. "Less suspicious that way. I mean, why would Amanda ever have a good reason for writing a check to me? But, writing it to Igor, if anyone found out, she could always say he was giving Lian extra lessons or something. God knows she could use some if she ever expects to win Nationals fair and square."

Bex admitted, "She did. That's what Amanda first said when I asked her. She said Igor was secretly giving Lian spinning lessons. It was only when I asked Lian about it that Amanda had to change her story."

"Yeah. I'd bet Lian didn't know what was going down. Mommy protects Lian from the big, bad scary world. It's kind of stupid, in a way. I mean, Amanda's got Lian convinced she's the best skater in the universe, no one's better and there's nothing she needs to work on. So, like, who can blame Lian for being totally surprised each time she doesn't win? Her mom, she's doing Lian a disservice. Building her up like that, only to have the judges tear her down. She'd do her a bigger favor if she said, hey, Lian, you're not too bad, and you're a hard worker, no one's arguing that; but your spins suck and that's why you keep being marked down in the technical and the presentation. Fix your spins and your in-betweens and maybe you'll see some better results. That's the way you get better, hearing the truth." Jordan shrugged again and added bitterly, "On the other hand, why bother when you can just buy the competition?"

"I'm sorry," Bex said.

"What the hell for?"

It wasn't that easy to explain. Bex only knew that something in Jordan's tone had prompted her spontaneous expression of sympathy. And it wasn't just condolence on not being able to buy her own competition. It actually had more to do with the wistfulness that had crept into Jordan's tone when she spoke about Amanda Reilly's devotion to her daughter's career.

Bex asked, "Do your parents ever come to watch you skate, Jordan?"

"My parents have better things to do."

"But they must have, when you were younger . . ."

"There's a reason I'm emancipated, okay? I don't need the hassle. You think I need somebody standing at the barrier with me at every practice, messing with my hair, shouting, 'You go, girl,' drying off my blades like I'm some paralyzed gimp who can't take care of herself?"

"I'm guessing the answer you're looking for is: no?"

"Just leave me alone, Bex. I still got to skate tonight. I got to focus."

"Okay." Bex nodded. "That's fine. Fair enough." She held out her hand. "Can I have my check back, please?"

"What do you mean, your check? It's my check, you just told me so yourself. It's my money. It's for me."

"But . . . but," Bex stammered, knowing that logic was the only weapon she had; as mentioned earlier, there wouldn't be any arm wrestling. "It won't do you any good. It's in Igor's name. You can't cash it without—"

Jordan grinned. "I know people."

And she was out the door. With Bex's evidence.

She really should be more careful with her irreplaceable evidence, Bex alternately flagellated and mused to herself. Especially when, despite what both Amanda and Jordan insisted, the complete story of the mysterious check seemed rather far from over. Jordan did not seem like the type to so easily agree to a fix, no matter how badly she needed the money. And even if a desperate Jordan had caved in, what about Igor? A coach was only as good as his last winning student. Would Igor really have allowed a skater with his name on her bio to skate badly? Was it possible, Bex mused (taking a break from the flagellation to grab a snack in the production office: tortilla chips and soda, mmm, mmm, good, a lunch of champions) that Jordan had accepted the deal before checking with Igor, and, when he found out, he put his foot down and forbade her from accepting Amanda's money? Would that be a motive for murder? On either Jordan's or Amanda's part?

It was certainly a train of thought worth pursuing.

And actually managing to hold on to the check sure would have made it easier.

Bex sighed. You'd think she'd be better at this by now. But her biggest problem seemed to be a sort of researcher's attention deficit disorder. She got so excited about one theory, that she dropped everything to untangle it . . . until the next theory came along, and there she went all over again.

Speaking of which—oh, look, there was Valeri Konstantin trying to sneak out and eat his own lunch in the hospitality suite set up for coaches and officials. Bex better quit musing about Jordan or Amanda killing Igor over a crooked deal gone sour and rush right over to pry out what Konstantin knew.

For one thing, he certainly knew more than Bex about where to get decent food at the arena. While she was still wiping tortilla crumbs from her jacket and tossing her soda can into the trash as she ran, he was sitting at a table covered with a white linen cloth and boasting a place setting of the china-and-metal—not plastic—variety. His plate was filled with plump, steaming beef and pork dumplings called *pelmeni* bobbing in vinegar and butter, while his non-plastic non-cup (it was a glass actually made out of . . . glass) seemed to be filled with a burgundy-colored, winelike substance. He was the only one sitting at his table. The handful of other coaches—all Russians; Gary was the sole American left at the competition and he'd made it quite clear to Bex how he felt about breaking bread with them—had circled their ice skates half a room away. Konstantin did not seem to mind the alone time. But Bex did. She plopped down next to him, trying not to salivate too visibly at his feast, and offered him her brightest smile.

Konstantin speared his *pelmeni* with a fork, took a bite, and ignored her.

She said, "I need to speak to you."

"It is dinner time. I am not working at this moment."

"That's okay, the particular time period I want to talk to you about, you weren't working then, either."

"This is about Marchenko?"

"Yes. How did you know?"

"You visited his mother and sister."

At the risk of sounding redundant. . . . "Yes. How did you know?"

"Friends," he said. "I have friends."

Which was exactly what Jordan had said about the check. Just a coincidence? Or was this conspiracy to kill Igor much broader than Bex could have imagined?

Bex said, "Igor's mother and sister, they told me some things. About you."

"Lies. Many, many lies."

"You're saying you and Alexandr Troika didn't harass them after Igor defected?"

"Igor Marchenko ruined the life of Alexandr Troika and myself. We were angry men. We have rights to be angry."

"Do you have the right to attack two women who never did anything to you?"

"Luba Marchenko, she had option to stop her son. When he is hiding at American embassy, she can speak to him, tell him not to do this, not to annihilate so many people. She did not do this. She is not innocent. The sister is not innocent."

"Luba and Sveta say you threatened them."

"A million years ago. Words said one million years ago, the memory lies."

"This was a week ago," Bex corrected. "They told me you called and threatened that something dire would happen if they came to the arena to see Igor."

"Nonsense."

"You didn't threaten them?"

"I did not threaten them. I did not call them. I have not engaged in contact with Igor's family for several years."

"Then why did they say you did?"

"Because they wish to make me look negative before reporter from television."

"That's possible, I guess."

"What do they say is my motive for this threat I did not make?"

"That you were afraid they'd tell the press about what you and Troika did to them after Igor defected."

"They have proof of this for press?"

"I—I don't know."

"I am not worried about what Marchenko family wishes to say about me. And I am also not worried"—he took a measured sip of wine and deigned to look up from his meal for the first time since Bex had come in—"about girl who works for television who is thinking I killed Igor Marchenko. I did not kill Igor Marchenko. I have no reason to kill Igor Marchenko. In Russia."

Now, there was a qualifier if Bex had ever heard one. "You mean you do have a reason to kill him somewhere else?"

"You think about this, Miss Researcher. I travel very much for competitions. I see Igor Marchenko many places in the world. If I wish to kill him, I kill him in another country, and then I get on plane and return to Russia. No one can arrest me. No one can do anything to me. But, in Russia, I am home. I cannot run away. So, you think about this. You think about this hard. Yes, Igor destroy my life for many, many years before I am able to get it back. Yes, I do not cry about his death. But, to kill Igor, I would not do this in Russia. It is stupid. And I am not stupid."

What a shame Bex could not say the same thing about herself.

Because, walking outside to check up on Sasha's progress tracking down Holistic Healing Man, Bex noted the following things: 1) Holistic Healing Man was not back; 2) The Gypsies with their crimson candy on a stick, however, were; and 3) Sasha was talking to them.

However: 4) Bex did not want Sasha talking to them, because she did not want them tipping off Holistic Healing Man; and 5) Perhaps Bex would have been more successful at getting Sasha to obey her wishes if she had taken the trouble to inform him of them first.

Well, it was too late now. The three seemed to be bosom buddies. Sasha spotted Bex across the street, called her name and enthusiastically, and waved her over.

"Bex, Bex, please to listen to this!"

Did she have a choice at this point? Bex crossed the street.

Sasha was crouching on the sidewalk next to the Gypsy couple. He said, "This is Nastia and this is her husband, German. They tell me something very interesting about the man who sells the medicine."

"I'm listening," Bex said, even as she wondered how they would ever catch up to the holistic healer if he first heard that someone was asking questions about him. Street vendors did not strike her as the type to enjoy a nice long chat about who they were, what they sold, and who might have purchased their wares for nefarious purposes.

"German and Nastia, they tell me the man who sells the medicine, he knows about Igor Marchenko. He is telling them last week—last week! Before Igor is killed!—he is telling them how Igor Marchenko was a boy and he defects. And then he tells them so many people are angry with Igor for leaving, he is surprised Igor risks return to Russia, because so many people, they probably want to kill him!"

"He told them this a week ago?" Bex wanted to make sure she was understanding correctly.

Sasha nodded fervently, practically bouncing up and down like a happy frog and looking so proud of his discovery that Bex almost forgave him. The problem was, she still hadn't figured out what she was mad at him for. But now wasn't the time to ponder that digression.

"How did he know?" Bex indicated the Gypsies. "Ask them, Sasha, please. Ask them how he knew anything about Igor Marchenko."

"Or perhaps . . ." The voice behind them made both Bex and Sasha jump in surprise. It did not sound friendly. Or happy. It did, however, sound very tall. And very close by. "Or, perhaps, you could ask him yourself."

Bex turned around. Although she wondered why she bothered. She already knew who would be standing there.

And he was tall.

And he was unhappy.

And he was holding a very large knife.

Eleven

Everything about him was very large. His navy blue, patched-on-both-elbows down coat loomed broadly at the shoulders and continued straight down, forming a rectangle topped by the triangle of fur that was his strapped hat. His black, rubber, fisherman-style boots went up until they disappeared into the folds of the coat. Even his ruddy mustache and beard were so lengthy it would have been impossible to determine where one ended and the other began, if it weren't for the unlit cigarette sticking from a slit somewhere to the left of his granite nose.

He would have been a gape-worthy sight under any circumstances. The foot-long knife that he clutched in both awkwardly gloved hands like a Samurai sword, however, did drive home the point (insert your favorite Vlad the Impaler guffaw, here) of his presence with particular . . . intensity.

For a moment, Bex could do nothing but obey instinct and gape mutely. She did notice, though, that Sasha, while doing the same, did, seemingly instinctively, also take a step forward. So that he now stood directly between Bex and Holistic Healing Man.

Not that his weapon wasn't long enough to pass right through Sasha on its way to Bex without so much as chipping the point.

But it was a noble gesture all the same.

Bex wondered if it was a lie or not.

"You have question for me?" To Bex's surprise, the voice that emerged from the mass of man wasn't the cavernous booming of a cartoon villain issuing orders from the darkness of his evil, echo-drenched lair. It was actually rather low; not exactly a whisper, more of a rumble. But perfectly controlled and in almost impeccable English.

Bex nodded, still waiting for her own voice to make a return appearance.

"Will you pay?" he asked.

She had exactly six hundred and seventeen rubles on her. Bex wasn't sure how much that translated to in dollars, but she knew that a piece of fruit, when you could find one at the market, started at fifty. So her total wasn't exactly flush bribery material.

Nevertheless, Bex nodded boldly. "How much do you want?"

He gave it some thought. "One hundred rubles."

Bex blessed the exchange rate.

She took Holistic Healing Man to a small coffee shop around the corner from the arena. She'd been meaning to dismiss Sasha, but he refused to leave her side. Or take his eyes off the knife. Even after Holistic Healing Man stuffed the weapon into the folds of his coat in response to Bex's teatime invitation, Sasha kept staring at the guy's pocket and twitching every time it looked like he might be reaching for his knife.

Once they got inside the eatery, though, Holistic Healing

Man seemed a lot less interested in his weapon than he was in the steaming cup of tea and the double-decker ham and brown bread sandwich Bex got him. He grabbed the ceramic cup with both hands and clutched it so tightly the skin all the way on the outside of his palms turned red. Bex could only imagine the blisters rising on the flesh in actual contact with the simmer.

For her part, she asked the indifferent woman at the counter for a bagel, figuring it best to stay away from meat of indeterminate origin, especially when there didn't seem to be a refrigeration case in sight.

Bex sat down at the metallic wicker table on the side next to Sasha, both of them facing Holistic Healing Man. The pair of them together seemed to take up as much space as one of him. He didn't remove his coat. Neither Bex nor Sasha invited him to.

Bex asked, "What's your name?"

"Fedya."

"Fed-yaw?" Bex repeated cautiously, breaking the name into two syllables and knowing she'd get it wrong anyway, but eager to demonstrate at least a token attempt at cultural sensitivity.

Sasha gently corrected, "No. Feh-d-yah. It is nickname. Short for Fedor."

"Hello, Fedya." Bex butchered his name for the second time. -

He might have chuckled in response. The slit between his beard and mustache twitched, and his massive shoulders bucked.

"How do you do?" he replied.

"You speak excellent English," she complimented.

"When I attended school, one foreign language was required to study. English, French, or German. I should have studied German. It is better for the study of medicine in University. But I very much enjoyed the books of James Fennimore Cooper. Cowboys and Indians. I wished to read them in their first language. Have you read these books?"

Bex admitted she hadn't.

"They do not teach them in school?"

"Not that I know off."

"Pity." He finished off his tea and grunted. When he let go off the cup, Bex saw that his palms were covered with calluses. So that's why the burning had so little effect. "My medicines," Fedya explained, "I grind for the medicine that I sell, it leaves marks on my hands." He mimed a small bowl and the turning of a pestle.

"That's what I wanted to talk to you about. Your medicines." Bex reached into her pocket and awkwardly pulled out a wad of bills. She wondered how one bribed properly. Was there an etiquette for this? Did she owe him the money before he talked, or after? Would he be offended if she did it wrong? Would giving money too late imply that she didn't trust him to keep his bargain? Would giving it too early show how out of her depth she was and prompt him to demand more?

She tallied what she had randomly plucked. Sixty rubles. Neither here nor there. She counted out fifty and laid them on the table in front of him. (Wasn't it illegal to bribe people in broad daylight? Wasn't it illegal to bribe people in general?) She said, "Half now, half when you've answered my questions."

There. That sounds reasonably hard-boiled.

Of course, now she didn't know what she was supposed to do with the leftover ten ruble note except roll it awkwardly around in her palm until it got mushy.

"More tea?" Sasha suddenly interrupted.

Bex thought that in addition to telling him that she didn't want him interviewing potential sources without her, she also should have told him not to interrupt when she was in the middle of a cross-examination. He was breaking her flow.

Fedya nodded and pushed his empty cup towards Sasha. Sasha stood up and, in one smooth gesture, picked up the cup, plucked Bex's ten rubles out of her hand, and headed towards the counter.

Okay. So the guy was useful. That last mental reprimand? Never mind.

Fedya took his money, recounted the bills, and tucked the wad in the general vicinity of his knife. "Your question," he prompted.

"It's about Igor Marchenko."

Fedya nodded, to indicate either that he'd heard of him, or merely that he'd heard her question. In any case, he didn't elaborate.

"The couple who sells their candy next to you?"

"It is poison," Fedya said.

"Really?"

She must not have been able to hide the shock on her face, because Fedya quickly explained, "Not arsenic, not hemlock, not the true poison, no. But what they paint candy with to make it the red color, it is chemical. It will not kill child who eats it dead. But, it is not good for the health."

"Oh," Bex said. And added one more iffy item to the list of foods she didn't feel like indulging in, in Russia. "But, anyway, the couple, they said that you told them about Igor Marchenko even before he was killed."

"Yes. This is true."

"How did you know about him? I mean, I guess his life story was probably in the Soviet papers when he first defected—"

"No. This is not true. Because, the Union of Soviet Socialist Republics, we learned from our teachers when we are growing up, is Socialist paradise where every person is happy all of the time. There can never be reason to leave Socialist Paradise, so no one ever wishes this. And if no one ever wishes this, then no one ever does this. And if no one ever does this, why would news and television to talk about this? When Igor wins the Olympics and they show us his skating on television, they tell us he is mentally deficient and that is why Americans are able to kidnap him and force him to skate for them. He is crazy. He is ill."

"Is that the story you told the Gypsy couple?" Bex asked, wondering if she were actually chasing a non-event here. When she heard that Fedya had told them about Igor, she'd jumped to the conclusion that he was telling them Igor's true story, and she wondered how he knew it before the newspapers had started rehashing it following his death. But if he was just telling the Gypsies something that he'd heard years ago on television, well, then there was nothing to investigate here at all. And Bex had spent one hundred rubles on nothing.

She wondered how she should phrase that for her expense report.

"No," Fedya said. "That is not the story I told them. They would not believe it, in any case. Now we know everything we hear on television then was lies." He paused, considering his words. "We knew it then, as well. We knew it was lies. But we did not have the imagination to guess what the truth was."

Sasha returned to their table, fresh tea in hand, just in time to catch Fedya's last words. He handed him the cup and glanced at Bex to check how she was absorbing her latest lecture on Russia's honesty problems. Bex deliberately did not meet his gaze.

"So how did you know the real truth about Igor's defection?"

"Because," Fedya took another sip of scalding tea. Wafting steam burned the tip of his nose, turning it pink above the mustache. "I was there."

"You were?" Bex blurted out the first thing that popped into to her mind. "Were you working for the KGB?"

Now, he definitely chuckled. It wasn't just a lip-slit here and a shoulder-buckle there. This time, the corners of his mouth actually turned up in amusement. He even set down his cup so that Bex might see his merriment.

Okay, she saw it. She just didn't get it. In her mind, Bex was too busy imagining Fedya as an ex-Communist spy, jobless and homeless since the collapse of the U.S.S.R. *The Spy Who Was Forced Into the Cold.*

"No. I was a medical student. A medical student who believed I was minding of my own business and sitting low, so no one noticed my existence. I thought I was safe."

"Fedor!" Sasha was interrupting her cross-examination, again. But, considering how helpful he'd been the last time, Bex decided to let him finish out his thought. "Sveta Marchenko's husband, his name, she says it was Fedor!"

"And he was a medical student!" Once given a big, ol' clue, Bex had no trouble fitting the rest of the pieces together. Could a person be both bright and delayed at the same time? Because that was her: eventually ingenious.

Fedya stretched out his arms and dipped his bushy head modestly, as if taking a bow of acknowledgement.

"That's how you knew Igor's real story!" Now that she'd been pointed in the right direction, Bex was all about stating the obvious.

"Yes."

She remembered, "Svetlana said you left her over what happened with Igor."

Fedya's hand, in what Bex could only hope was a subconscious, nervous tick, traveled to his pocket. He patted the knife, as if soothing it. "Yes."

"She said you both were thrown out of the university. That you lost your home, that your friends refused to be seen with you."

His hand paused, squeezing the knife's hilt. "Yes. Yes, this happened."

Bex recalled what Konstantin said about Luba having the power to stop Igor's defection if she'd wanted to, and asked

Fedya, "Did you blame Svetlana for what happened to you?"

"I blamed Sveta and Luba for raising such a spoiled boy, that he does not think of how his selfish actions will affect others. They treat him like he is a prince. A king. Igor is athlete, Igor is special. Igor is allowed to do what he wants. He hears this all his life, so of course Igor does not stop to think before he defects. Igor wishes to go to America, the rest of us can die, thank you."

"So you blamed Igor."

"Igor *is* to blame."

Bex spoke slowly, the sentence forming after the words were already said. Which probably wasn't the best way to go about asking a loaded question, especially considering what Bex heard herself proposing. "So, you blamed Igor for your not being able to finish medical school. And now you make homeopathic medicine. And Igor was killed with a homeopathic version of digitalis. And you knew he was at the arena."

That did it. This time, Fedya went whole-hog and laughed out loud.

He laughed so loudly, even the indifferent waitress raised her chin long enough to shush him angrily. Fedya glared back at her and made a vague threatening gesture with the sweep of one, massive arm. She got the message and went back to indifference.

"You think that I poisoned Igor?"

"You had means. You had opportunity. You had motive."

"I also have a mind that has not, thank you, gone senile. Igor Marchenko already destroyed me once. Why do you think I would allow him to do so again?"

Bex had no reason to believe him. Except that she also had no non-circumstantial evidence to the contrary.

"Alright," she said, putting his denial on the back burner for now. "Then maybe you can answer this for me." To stress her point, Bex reached into her pocket and gave him the remaining fifty rubles. Igor's one-time brother-in-law stuffed the cash into his other pocket. The non-lethal one. Bex asked, "How long have you been selling holistic medicine outside the arena?"

Fedya shrugged. "Several years. Maybe five, six. It is a good location. People who work around come to me regularly, every month, every week. I make very excellent medicine. Working medicine, strong. But it is also good location because so many new people come to arena often. For competitions and shows and important meetings. I have many new customers all the time."

Bex asked, "Did you have any new customers the last few days? I mean, since the skating competition started?"

"Yes. Some. The little girl with the auburn, curly hair, she came to me. She had pains. A fight, she said. She bought ointment I make. Very good for pains."

"Did anyone come to you asking for digitalis?"

"No." Fedya shook his head definitely.

Well. There went that whole line of questioning. If Fedya was telling the truth, Bex had just hit a brick wall. Unless he himself was the murderer, she would get nothing she could use to solve the mystery here.

"The girl who bought it, she was not asking for digitalis."

Wait. Rewind.

"The girl who bought what?" Bex quizzed.

"It is a powder I make, for muscle illness. It is helpful when muscles are hard or they are frozen, cramping."

"What does this have to do with digitalis?"

"The muscle medicine, it is very, very expensive to make. To recoup my money, I need to sell muscle medicine along with other medicine. Cheap to make medicine. So they balance out. The girl, she asks me only for the muscle medicine, but she buys set of three, because I will not sell to her otherwise. She buys muscle medicine one, belladonna for digestion two, and three, digitalis."

Bex prayed. She prayed very hard. And then she asked.

"Do you remember who the girl was? Did she tell you her name?"

"No. No, she did not tell me her name." Fedya attempted a joke. "I do not take credit cards on the street, so I do not ask for—what is the word?—proper identification. But I know it is the American skater. With the golden hair. The one who is Igor's student, so I know her name. Like the Arab country. It is Jordan."

Twelve

Bex thanked Fedya. Bex thanked him profusely. That too seemed to amuse him, but Bex no longer cared if he had a laugh at her expense. Heck, he could have an entire fit of hysteria for all she cared. Because if Fedya was telling the truth . . .

She thanked him again. She bought him another cup of tea. And then, before he left, she got up the courage to ask, "Fedya, excuse me, but why do you carry a knife?"

"Bandits," he said simply, and as if it were the most logical answer in the world. "I sell on the street for anyone to see, and I only accept money in cash. There are many who would like to rob me. I need protection. This is a very dangerous city. A dangerous country. This is difficult for you to understand. We are a difficult people to understand."

He tipped his hat to Bex. He nodded briskly to Sasha, and then he was gone. Bex watched him trudge down the snowy street. And she remembered his idea of an alibi for Igor's murder. "I also have a mind that has not, thank you, gone senile." It was awfully reminiscent of Valeri Konstantin's, "I am not stupid." Why did everyone think she was insulting their intelligence? She was just doing her job, after all.

And, in the interest of being thorough, Bex asked Sasha, "Did you believe him?"

She recognized the irony of her query. Here she'd spent half the day pouting because Sasha had intimated he might not always be honest with her—or, rather, that he wouldn't hesitate to be dishonest should the need come up, which was somewhat different, she supposed—and now she was asking him to judge Fedya's veracity.

"Did you?" Sasha politically popped the ball right back into her court. This boy would go far in show business.

"I don't know. I mean, yeah, he acted like my suggesting he'd poisoned Igor was the most ridiculous thing in the world. But he didn't seem that surprised when I brought it up. Also, I bet because he's been around the neighborhood for so long, nobody would have noticed if he popped into the arena. Maybe he even does it all the time, he says he has regular customers there. And who better than the guy who makes the drug to know exactly how much to administer it to make sure the dose is lethal? And he has a big reason to hate Igor. On paper, he's the most logical suspect. And there's one more thing. I've been thinking about this since Valeri Konstantin claimed he didn't make those telephone calls threatening Luba and Sveta. Maybe someone else made them, and just said they were Konstantin. So if that's the case, why would somebody do that? I figure they did it to keep Luba and Sveta from coming down to the arena. Like, maybe Fedya was the one who did it, because he didn't want them to recognize him. He said he likes to fly under the radar in general. And you'd definitely want that if you were going to kill somebody. You wouldn't want anyone around who could draw unnecessary attention to you."

"His story about Jordan buying digitalis, you think this is a lie?"

"Only one way to find out," Bex said. And hailed a cab for the official hotel.

Jordan opened her door dressed only in an oversized T-shirt with the words, "U.S. Figure Skating Team" written on it in red, white, and blue. It may have been more than the bra and panties she'd donned for her and Bex's first conversation two days earlier, but it was still revealing enough to show off the tautness of her stomach and the leanness of her thighs and arms.

Bex was happy that she'd prompted Sasha to stay down the hall and chat up the floor matron again, instead of accompanying her to Jordan's room. He didn't need to see how attractive she was. It would distract him.

Yeah. That was it. Distract him.

Bex asked, "Can we chat for a couple of minutes, Jordan?"

"Uhm . . . I was kind of getting ready for bed."

The clock read seven P.M. which, for a normal skater, actually was bedtime. Frankly, it was somewhat past, considering most normal skaters got up at four A.M. to hit the rink before everyone else got there. But, Jordan was hardly a normal skater. She was a renowned, self-proclaimed party animal. Most parties, in Bex's, granted, limited experience, tended to start after seven P.M., didn't they?

"This won't take long." She invited herself inside.

Jordan's hotel room looked just like Bex's identical room a few floors below. One bed, one nightstand, a lamp, an old-fashioned rotary phone, and a TV hidden in the wardrobe. The color scheme was a muted brown, making the borrowed clothing rack in the corner, from which hung Jordan's sequined, neon pink, green and canary yellow skating dresses the inescapable focal point. Which was the only reason Bex even noticed the damp-cloth–covered ironing board next to the dresses, and the steaming iron, recently unplugged for safety and standing on its side. Somehow, the image of Jordan diligently ironing her performance costumes the night before competition struck Bex as incongruous with the rest of her persona.

Reluctant to jump right in with, "So, Jordan, isn't it interesting that you happened to buy a poison that, a day later, happened to kill your coach?" Bex decided to ease into the harder questions by opening with, "So, Jordan, any luck cashing Igor's check?"

Jordan shrugged and plopped down on the bed, Indian-style. "I'm doing okay."

Bex realized it was the first time she'd ever seen Jordan without makeup. At the major international events it was unofficially compulsory that the girls, and sometimes the boys, too, wear make-up even to practice sessions. And Bex only ever saw Jordan in practice or in competition. She had no idea there was actual skin under the layers of foundation, powder, tint, blush, lipstick, mascara, eye shadow and sparkle-dust. Rather young skin, at that. Sitting Indian-style on the bed, dressed only in a T-shirt, her face bare, Jordan looked more like a teen at a slumber party than an international athlete, a Madison Avenue spokesperson, and a possible cold-blooded killer.

But, one thing at a time, Bex.

She kept up the casual chatter. "You been okay, practicing without a coach?"

"Sure. I mean, what's he going to tell me twenty-four hours before a competition that he shouldn't have told me a million times beforehand?"

"Well, there's also the emotional support."

"I'm a big girl. I don't need anybody holding my hand."

"So I guess his death didn't affect you much?"

"Yeah, you know, whatever. Easy come, easy go." Jordan's head bobbed up and down, causing the bedsprings to creak.

Bex asked, "Jordan, what do you know about holistic medicine?"

The bedsprings stopped creaking. Jordan's head stopped mid-bob. She glared at Bex. She said, "How'd you figure it out?"

Was that a confession? Bex had been expecting obfuscation, denial, feigned confusion. She hadn't been expecting . . . was that a confession?

Bex stammered, "I—I did some research. That's my job, you know. And—"

"It's none of your business. It's private."

"Actually, Jordan, I think anybody's business would extend to—"

"And it's not against the rules! I checked!"

Bex shut her mouth. She opened it again to slowly ask, "Jordan, do you think the rules in Russia against murder are that different from U.S. law?"

"Murder? What are you talking about, murder?"

"Igor Marchenko—"

"Who's talking about Igor? I'm talking about earlier today, when you saw me with the cigar and the arnica."

"What's arnica?"

"It's just an ointment for sore muscles and bruises, that's it. It doesn't have any banned substance in it. I checked. It's totally legal. And the cigar, it's not even tobacco; so it's definitely not pot or any bad stuff like that. I just light it and apply the heat to my pressure points, on my knees, mostly. It's therapeutic."

"You think I'm here to bust you over some stuff you use on your knees?"

"Well, the stupid ISU has their bunch of stupid rules about what you can and can't use when you're competing. Remember that Chinese chick that got her medal taken away because of cough medicine, for Pete's sake? I didn't want to risk it."

"So, then, why use the . . . what did you call it? Arnica?"

"Because it works. It works better than the prescription crap that they charge you an arm and a leg and a couple of hips for. And I'm not exactly swimming in money. I've got to work with what I've got."

Bex said, "Jordan, I'm not here to talk about muscle cream."

"Then what's with the homeopathic questions?"

"Jordan," Bex took a deep breath. "There is a man. He sits outside the arena. He sells homeopathic medicine."

"Yeah, so?"

"He told me he sold you some of his medicine the other day. He told me he sold you digitalis. The same drug that killed Igor."

"He's a liar!" Jordan attempted to leap off the bed, but she tripped, and ended up more hopping forward, still on her knees.

"You didn't buy anything from him?"

"I didn't buy digitalis!"

"You didn't?"

"I mean, I did . . . damn it!" Jordan yanked a pillow out from under the bedspread and hugged it her chest, like body armor. It was white with dark blue stripes. Prison-style. Bex tried not to get lost in the symbolism. "I only bought the dig-italis because the bastard wouldn't sell me what I really needed without it. Wait, look, I'll show you." She success-fully made it off the bed, stomped to her closet, dug around under a pile of mashed sweaters and pants which, in contrast to the neatly ironed skating dresses, just lay in a heap on the floor, and pulled out a wooden case. The black and white checkered squares suggested it had once been a chess set, but had been re-purposed. Jordan brought the case to the bed, laying it down extra-carefully with both hands, like a wobbly-headed baby. She snapped open the gold-plated locks and turned the holder to face Bex, so that she could see for herself the twelve five-ounce bottles lined up six by six, one on top of the other. Four of the clear glass bottles were filled with blue liquid, four with green, and four with brown.

Jordan indicated the brown ones. "This is the digitalis. See, they're all still full. That shows I didn't use them on Igor, or on anybody. Doesn't it?"

Bex pointed out, "All the bottles are still full. They haven't even been opened."

"So? Doesn't that prove my point that I didn't kill him?"

"You said you bought the muscle-pain stuff for your knees. You said I caught you using it earlier. You haven't used any of this, as far as I can see."

"This isn't arnica. It's something else. Arnica is usually an ointment. At least, that's how I use it. I slather it on before practice and after."

"So what's this for?"

Jordan hesitated.

"Is *this* the illegal substance you thought I'd found out about?"

"No! No, I mean, this isn't even for mc.

"Who is it for, then?"

"It's for . . ." Jordan looked away, pondering either the dresses or the iron, or just the cruel world at large. When she looked back, she asked, "Promise you won't tell?"

"Depends," Bex hedged. If this was something illegal, immoral—or, more importantly, something 24/7 needed to make their coverage more interesting—she didn't want to be stuck in a pinkie-swear.

"It's got nothing to do with skating. Honest."

"Well, if it's got nothing to do with skating . . ."

"It's for my dad," Jordan said.

"Your dad. You have a dad?"

"You think I hatched from a pod?"

"No, but, I mean . . ."

"I know what you mean. No one's seen my parents for years. I want it that way."

"Why?"

"Because," Jordan said. "Because of people like you."

"People like me?"

"Yes. People like you. TV people, newspaper people. Why can't you guys just let us skate, and that's it? Who cares what we think about world peace, or what we had for breakfast, or whether our parents have any cinematic diseases for you to exploit like it's a movie of the week or something."

That last part seemed to offer too many details to be just a hypothetical rant. Bex asked, "Do they? Your parents? Do they have any cinematic diseases?"

"My dad," Jordan said, "he has ALS. That's Lou Gehrig's disease. You know, like that Stephen Hawkins guy, the physicist? He's almost totally paralyzed. Couple of years now. He can't walk. He can't talk. My mom takes care of him all by herself."

"I'm sorry," Bex said.

"Yeah. But not too sorry, I bet, to turn it into a sappy up-close-and-personal, full of close-ups where my dad's got food dripping down his chin or my mom's changing his sheets, and I'm skating at the rink with something lame like 'Wind Beneath My Wings' playing over the whole scene."

She had a point. And it was eerily accurate.

"So you pretend you don't have any parents at all."

"I don't pretend. I happen to really be legally emancipated. I've got the papers. And that's all I told the press. You guys made up the rest, about how I don't speak to my parents and all the other crap."

"So the medicine is for your dad?"

"Yeah. My mom and I did some research, and there's really good evidence that it can help him. But it's illegal to make in the U.S. So when I knew I was going to Russia, I told her I'd bring some back. It's not illegal here. They sell it on the street, duh."

"Along with digitalis."

"I told you I only bought the digitalis because that Shylock forced me! I didn't get it to kill Igor, and I certainly didn't use it to kill Igor! Why the hell would I do that? They guy was like, nicer to me than anyone, ever. He knew all about my dad being sick. He knew my mom barely had money to pay his doctor bills, so she certainly wasn't going to be shelling out for my stupid skating. That's why Igor didn't charge me anything for my lessons. He hasn't charged me in maybe two years." Jordan sighed. She looked at Bex. She said, "And you know, what? I was such a bitch to him. When Igor first told me he wouldn't charge me, I was like: 'What's the catch? You want me to put out for you or something?' God, what a pain in the ass. Igor told me: 'No catch.' He said somebody once did him a major favor without asking for anything in return, and this was his way of paying it back. Or, well, paying it forward, I guess. Anyway, I've got no reason to kill Igor. I'm up shit-creek without him. Who the hell is going to coach me now? I don't have the money for a Gary Gold or a Lucian Pryce or someone like that. I would have been an idiot times a thousand if I'd killed Igor. And if you don't believe me, you go ask your favorite source, Mrs. Reilly."

Bex felt like her grasp on the conversation had just hit the ground with a thud. "Amanda Reilly? What does Amanda Reilly have to do with any of this?"

"Amanda knows Igor was giving me free lessons. She knows that I don't have any other money. That's why she's been paying all my expenses for the last year."

Thirteen

"It's true," Amanda said. Well, technically, she said "It's true" after ten minutes of swearing that it wasn't. But, as Bex went through her infinite collection of skeptical faces, she eventually broke down and confessed.

"You've been paying Jordan's expenses for the past year?"

"Just her ice-time. And her costumes and travel. But not her lessons. Igor was giving her those for free."

"So that's what your check to Igor was about? It was for Jordan's expenses?"

"Yes."

"Not so that she would take a dive at nationals."

"No."

"So when Jordan confirmed your story. Your first story, 1 mean, she was just—"

"I'm sure she needed the money. Maybe she thought she could cash it."

"So, you were lying, and Jordan was lying, when you

both swore to me the money was for her taking a dive? But neither Jordan nor you are lying now, when you say it was for Jordan's skating expenses?"

"Yes."

"And I should believe you, because . . . ?"

"Because"—Amanda tossed her hands up in the air, then allowed them to fall to her sides with an audible thwack—"because I'm tired, Bex. Because I'm tired of all this, and I'm tired of all that, and I'm tired, darn tired, of figure skating."

Did the sun get tried of shining? Did snow get tired of falling? Did rainbows get tired of . . . uhm, raining?

A skating mother tired of skating? There was no such animal as far as Bex knew.

"I'm not sure I understand," she offered in place of, "Huh, what now?"

"It's so hard, Bex. Did you know Lian and I moved to Connecticut so that she could skate with Gary? I have a husband. Yes. Nobody knows that, because it's always Lian and me at practice and Lian and me at competitions, but I do have a husband. He's back home. Which means I'm the one taking care of Lian, 24/7." Amanda smiled at her unintentional evocation of Bex's employer. "Yes, 24/7. I drive Lian to the rink every morning at six A.M. I sit in the stands for three hours, and then I drive her to school. I pick her up after school and drive her to ballet lessons, then back to the rink. Then I drive her home. I watch her diet and make her costumes and I answer her fan mail and I make her travel arrangements. I travel with her and spend my days either at the rink or at the hotel. Would you believe I went to Paris and didn't see the Louvre? We went to Italy and I never saw the Vatican. I play interference with Lian and the press. I help her write out what to say so that she always comes off sounding well, and I keep clippings for her scrapbooks, and I make sure she's not overlooked in favor of . . . flashier . . . skaters."

"Like Jordan Ares." Bex pointed out the obvious.

"Lian thinks she is always being overlooked in favor of Jordan." Amanda sighed.

"I think my follow-up question is kind of a gimme by this point. But I could spell it out for you, if you'd like."

Amanda took the liberty of doing that for her. "You want to know why I've been financially supporting my daughter's biggest competitor."

"That would be nice."

"Because I am very, very much ready for an end to all of . . . this." Amanda waved her arm vaguely, indicating, perhaps, the entire skating universe. "To be honest, I was ready the day Lian took her first private skating lesson. I didn't mind the group ones so much. Yes, it was awfully cold at the rink and I found it pretty boring, not to mention how much it hurt me personally every time my Lian fell. But, at least I had other mothers there to chat with. It was rather social and friendly and low-key, if you can believe it."

"But, that's not how it is in big-time skating."

"Big-time skating!" Amanda snorted. "That's not how it is in pre-preliminary girls, ages four to five, group B, compulsory moves! The moment you step on that horrible USFSA competitive track, everything changes. Women who you foolishly thought were your friends—well, at least friendly acquaintances—now that your child is in competition with theirs, are suddenly not even sitting next to you at the rink, much less chatting! Suddenly, everything is life or death. I hate it. I've hated it for years."

"So why do you keep doing it then?"

"Because. Lian loves it. It makes her happy. She loves to compete and she loves to win and she even loves to practice. She can be in the foulest of moods, but all we have to do is come to the rink, Lian takes a deep breath, she puts on her skates, she steps on the ice and she's off. Free. Happy. My little girl. Who didn't even smile her first year with us. My little baby Lian. Skating is her world. I couldn't tell her to quit, I just couldn't. She'd never speak to me, again. And if that happened, Bex, I would die."

"So where does Jordan fit into all of this?"

"Jordan was my way out. Or, at least, I was hoping she would be. This past year, Bex, this year has been the worst one yet. Ever since Erin Simpson announced that she was retiring and left the National title open—not that she could have stayed in skating anyway, after what happened with her mother and that horrible murder incident—Lian has been obsessed—even more than she usually is—with winning. She's doubled her training time. Skating is all she talks about, all she thinks about. She's like . . . like . . . like sort of a zombie. I look at her and I think, this can't be right. This can't be good for her, I must be making a mistake. It got to the point where I could barely stand it. I was crying every day, I was under so much stress. I was so worried about what this was doing to my baby. But I couldn't muster the courage to tell her to stop. I couldn't do it, Bex. After a while, even Lian noticed how upset I was. She asked me what was wrong. She really is a sweet girl. You just can't tell right now, because she's so focused on her skating. But she can be the most loving daughter. When she has time to be."

Bex nodded. To indicate that she was following the story. Because she certainly wasn't believing it.

"She asked me what was wrong," Amanda continued. "And I told her. Well, not everything. I just told her how worried I was about her, that she was working so hard, and I was worried what would happen, well, what would happen if she didn't achieve her goals. Was she putting all this work in for nothing? What if she didn't win Nationals this year? Would she keep going? Keep going at this same pace? What if she didn't win for several years? What if she never won? When would she decide enough is enough?"

"And Lian didn't mind you asking that? I mean, it doesn't sound very, you know, supportive? It sounds like you don't think Lian can win. Didn't that make her mad?"

"It did. She told me she just knew this was her year. This was the year she was going to win Nationals. Maybe even Worlds, too. At least, she thought this was her year to medal at Worlds. So that's when we made our deal. If Lian wins Nationals, we keep going the way we've been going. For as long as she wants. I'll go along with it, because, if she wins Nationals, that means Lian knows what she's doing and where she's going. But, if she doesn't win this year, then we quit. Cold turkey. No more. We quit and we leave Connecticut and we go home to stay. She can skate on the weekends. For fun. But no more competing. She can go to college. She can be normal."

"And this way, her quitting isn't your fault."

"We made a deal," Amanda insisted. "I'm not the one making her quit. It's not me she should be angry at if things don't work out. We made a deal. She agreed."

"It was a good deal on your part," Bex agreed. "Lian has never beaten Jordan in any competition, national or international. Odds are, Jordan's going to win Nationals, too."

"But only if she has the money to keep training," Amanda reminded her.

"Which is where you came in."

"Jordan was my only chance. I couldn't let her quit. I went to Igor, and we made a deal. I wrote the checks to him. I couldn't write them to Jordan. Now, though, now I don't know what I'm going to do. Has Jordan hinted to you who her new coach might be? She's not thinking of switching to Gary, is she? Because, I don't think Gary would go along with this. Well, he might go along with me paying for Jordan, but he wouldn't agree to not telling Lian. You know Gary, he's so proper and honorable. No impropriety with him. He won't let us, if we run into a judge at the hotel restaurant, totally by accident, he won't let us treat them to a dinner or breakfast or, heck, even a cup of coffee. He says it wouldn't look right. But you know everyone else is doing it!"

Bex said, "So, actually, you had no motive for killing Igor."

"Of course not! Igor was helping me. Naturally, I know he was doing it for his own reasons. Of course he wanted Jordan to keep skating, and with Lian out of the way, Jordan would be the undisputed number one American lady, no competition. So, it's not like he was doing me any favors out of the goodness of his heart. But I certainly would have no reason to kill him!"

Lian, on the other hand, Bex couldn't help thinking, just got another one.

Back at the Bolshoi Theater, Lian had acted surprised to learn about her mother writing checks to Igor. But, Lian also "acted" out the role of a fiery, Spanish temptress in her short program (music from *Carmen*) and that of a melancholy, dying feline (music from *Cats*) in her long. So "lying little girl" wouldn't be that much of stretch. If even Amanda was afraid of what her "loving daughter—when she has time" would do to her if she found out Mommie Dearest was bankrolling the despised competition, what might she do to the coach who'd made it all possible?

It was an interesting question, and one that warranted more investigation.

If only Bex's day job wasn't getting in the way.

The ladies' short program was set to begin in less than an hour. And Bex was needed in the TV announcer's booth, where Francis and Diana Howarth's respective tongues might not have been as deadly as Fedya's trusty knife, but they were certainly as sharp. And, in the opinion of the 24/7 legal department, just as dangerous.

Bex planted Sasha outside the rink-side booth's door, with orders to keep curious passersby from poking their heads in while 24/7 was on the air. Then she mouthed a silent apology to the cameraman as she ducked beneath his scope and stepped over his cables to take her seat between Francis and Diana (she'd determined that they argued less, if they had to make the effort of actually leaning either behind or in front of Bex to stick their tongues out at each other). In a rare bit of synchronicity, both had remembered to bring their research binders. Diana was using hers to prop up her compact mirror as she applied her mascara. Francis was fanning himself under the hot camera lights with the plastic cover to his. But at least Bex wouldn't have to make her customary mad dash back to their dressing rooms to retrieve the binders from underneath a pile of makeup and discarded clothes. Maybe this was a good omen. Maybe it meant they would have an easy show.

Francis asked Bex, "How many skaters, in total, have previously taken the ice in an international competition without a coach?"

"And how many of those skaters were Americans?" Diana added.

Okay. So much for good omens.

"I don't know," Bex told them honestly. Prior to the competition, she had remembered to compile a list of skaters who were born in one country but skated for another; skaters who competed against other skaters from their same training site; World Junior Champions (Singles, Ladies, Pairs and Dance—why presume that this being a ladies only event would somehow quench Francis's childlike sense of delightful curiosity) who went on to become World Champions; skaters who were emancipated minors; and skaters who were adopted . . . But, she had neglected to research how many skaters ever competed without a coach.

"I'm disappointed in you, Bex." Francis sniffed.

Diana just shook her head sadly. Obviously too crushed for words.

Bex took her seat between America's former sweethearts and looked at her show rundown, the televised order in which the ladies would be skating, tonight. Although, technically, the competition draw was always supposed to be random, the fact that there were only four skaters in the entire event and, more importantly, that this was a made-for-TV show, meant that Gil had gotten to select the order for maximum audience building. He'd decided that Lian would go first, since she was American and nobody wanted fans who were just tuning in to think this would be a show full of foreigners. Then Brittany, because even though she was skating for Russia, she was really an American and could answer her post-skating questions without any silly accent. Then Galina, because, well, she did have to skate sometime. But they could use her program to tease that Jordan was coming up next, which is who everybody really wanted to see, anyway. Not only was she the bad girl of skating, but, now, her coach was dead! Murdered! What luck! So, while in the interest of journalistic integrity, they wouldn't be announcing on the air that this particular draw was random, they wouldn't exactly be doing anything to correct the misconception, either.

Bex looked around the arena, which was filling up gradually with a Russian hum that turned into a buzz, that turned into a verbal borscht. The crowd, she was intrigued to note, looked a great deal like the one she'd seen previously at the Bolshoi. Instead of the comfy jeans, one-size-fits-all down jackets and multi-colored sweatshirts festooned with their favorite skater's silk-screened action photo that were de rigueur at American arenas, this crowd had come as dressed up for a night of skating as they would for the ballet. The women wore long skirts, expensive blouses, and high-heeled shoes that made climbing steps to the higher levels particularly challenging. Many of the men, both young and old, wore suits. They followed dutifully behind their respective women, clutching bouquets of flowers ready to be flung onto the ice, so that the women's hands were free to hold on to the stairway's railing. That, at least, was exactly like the audience in America. This was still a woman's sport. The men were only dragged to it.

"There are certainly a lot of Russians, here," Francis offered what, Bex bet, could already qualify as the front-runner for her Ultimate Inanity of the Night Award. But then, he added, "I expected a capital city like Moscow to have attracted more of the former Soviet Union's ethnic minorities. Kazakhs, Uzbeks, Turks, Armenians, Moldavians . . ." And Bex realized that, no, as usual, she was the inane one.

"Why," Diana demanded, "would you have expected that, you silly goat? The Soviets did their best to wipe out whatever individuality those ethnic groups had. They closed their schools, made them all speak Russian, forcibly deported half of them to other republics to keep them from putting together a rebellion. . . . What in the world makes you think any of them would want to stay in Moscow once their own homelands were freed?"

"Do you honestly believe that after spending a lifetime in a cosmopolitan city like Moscow, there would be a mad rush to return to a third world republic, regardless of your ethnic origin? How do you keep them on the farm once they've seen the Kremlin?"

"The Kremlin . . . Lubjanka prison . . . Ah, yes, what wonderful memories they must harbor of the good old Soviet days . . ."

It was a half-hour to showtime, and they were already arguing. About politics, no less. This could only be a harbinger of great things to come.

Bex slipped on her headset, hoping to shut out the Howarth version of *Crossfire—On Ice!* It worked, in as much as she couldn't hear Francis and Diana anymore. Instead, Bex got the radio-drama known as "Gil Cahill Rallies the Troops in the Truck." As far as rousing pep talks went, it was no Saint Crispin's Day Speech. It wasn't even "Win one for the Gipper." Gil Cahill's idea of getting his employees pumped to go live on the air was to stand at the back of the production truck, headset on his head, all keys open lest anyone miss a word, and issue random orders, preferably without identifying whom he was speaking to first. The better, Bex guessed, to keep everyone on their toes and paying attention to each barked missive. After all, any fool could tune out the din and merely obey an order that was addressed to them by name. But 24/7 employees were special. They all did a little mind reading on the side.

"Cue tape. . . . Bring up audio. . . . Let me see the graphic page. . . . Cut audio. . . . That music sucks, don't you have anything less gay? . . . Camera One, did I ask for a fucking shot of the fucking wall? Talent, test your mikes. . . . I said, test your mikes, dammit!"

Oh, wait. That last order was for her. Because, while Bex may not have been the "talent" Gil was speaking to (he would never dream of calling anyone not on-camera any such thing), her proximity to the actual "talent," Francis and Diana, meant that it was her responsibility to not only provide their research material, but also to baby-sit. As neither had their headset on at the moment—they were too busy debating who was really to blame for the Armenia/Azerbaijan conflict—it was up to Bex to pass on the message that Gil wished for them to say a few words into the microphone so that their audio man could set sound levels.

"If Gorbachev, as part of his reforms, had only decided to right the wrongs of forcible population transfer"—Francis allowed Bex to wedge the headset over both of his ears, without breaking stride—"that entire ethnic conflict could have been avoided!"

"Fifty years after the fact"—Diana chose to put on her own headset; after all, her hairstyle was at stake—"is too late to make up for past wrongs. People forged new homes for themselves in the areas where they had been resettled. Moving them back to a place most of them have never been to is tantamount to another forced transfer!"

"Okay, that's good, guys." Gil crackled from the truck. And then he asked Bex, "Is that history you wrote them for the show? Because, you know, this politics shit is way over most people's heads at home." Then, again to no one in particular, he announced, "It's showtime, gang! Let's see who can screw up the least on this go-around."

With encouragement like that, Bex thought as she opened both Francis's and Diana's binders and indicated where they were in the rundown, *how could they fail?*

Fourteen

In the "Thank God for small favors" column, the poor, displaced Azerbaijanis and Armenians were forgotten the instant the 24/7 camera's red light clicked on in the booth, indicating Francis and Diana were live on the air. On the "But, then again . . ." side, both now had all this contrary energy pent up. And nowhere to spew it except the ice.

They didn't even wait for Lian Reilly to strike her opening pose before putting up their proverbial dukes. She was still skating to the center, dressed in a crimson dress with plunging, lacy cleavage, and a rose pinned to her jet-black hair in a not-too-successful attempt at helping a tiny Asian girl impersonate a hot-blooded, Spanish temptress, when Francis fired off: "Lian Reilly is, without a doubt, the weak link of this competition. She has neither the grace and presentation of a Jordan Ares or Brittany Monroe, nor the multi-revolution jumps of Galina Smetanova."

He'd managed to confuse Galina's real name, Semenova,

with the Russian word for sour cream. But that wasn't why Gil shrieked, "Stop it!"

He'd meant Francis, but the headset he chose to howl the command into was Bex's. Gil never addressed the talent directly in the middle of a live broadcast. They sometimes forgot to hit the mute button before talking back.

"Bex! Stop him! Friggin' show's barely started and he's telling people this brat's not worth their attention. We got to keep them watching another hour. Positive energy! Now, now, now!"

On the ice, Lian was opening her program with some brusque head turns and toe taps accompanied by feisty swishes of her skirt. It looked to Bex like she was dusting the flounces. Bex scribbled furiously on an index card and held it up for Francis and Diana to see. The card read: "Gil says—Talk about something else!!!! Now!!!!"

Diana read the note, snuck a mischievous peek at Francis, and opened her mouth.

Bex held up another card. It read: "Not about Armenia."

Diana closed her mouth, disappointed.

Bex's third card read, "Be POSITIVE!!!!"

Francis said, "Lian Reilly, Diana, is certainly one of the brightest up-and-coming skating stars in America."

Bex had to hand it to the man. Not only had he managed to completely contradict his previous statement without so much as a gulp in between, he also made it sound like it was actually Diana who'd spouted the earlier negativity about Lian, and Francis had been defending her all along.

But this wasn't Diana's first time at the skating rodeo, either. She shot back with, "Then why in the world, Francis, would you label her the weak link of this competition?"

Francis said, "Diana, the death of coach Igor Marchenko has certainly cast a pall over this entire event."

"What is this?" Gil demanded of Bex over the headset. "A Harold Pinter play?"

Bex was wondering the same thing. Were Francis and

Diana planning to utter declarative statements with no connection to each other for the rest of the broadcast?

Diana replied, "It certainly has, Francis. And I am sure
we will see the effects of that death reflected in each of the
young ladies' performances tonight."

Okay, that was better. They were actually having a semblance of a conversation. Albeit a morbid one.

"It certainly will be a unique night of skating," Francis
mused.

"Oh, yes." Diana couldn't wait to agree more. "We'll be
seeing history made. No skaters in our sport's history have
ever competed under such circumstances before."

Bex shuddered, as if someone had scraped their teeth
against a chalkboard while walking over her grave on Friday
the thirteenth. She'd asked and pleaded and begged Francis
and Diana never, ever to make an absolute statement without letting her research the facts first. All she needed was for
Gil to receive a letter from some uber-fan salivating that in
1972 at a junior skating event in the mountains of Yu-
goslavia, the coach of the Rumanian team tripped and hit her
head, leaving her entire squad to compete as orphans and,
Jesus, what kind of researchers did 24/7 hire that they didn't
know such a basic fact?

Diana was aware of Bex's need to vet all information before it went out on the air. Which was why, as she made her
unsubstantiated absolute statement, she turned her head towards Bex and shrugged apologetically. As if she had no
idea what in the world had possessed her to say such a thing,
but who was she to argue with an impulse?

"Of course, the skater most likely to be affected," Francis
offered the obvious, "is Jordan Ares. She was Igor's student,
you know."

At that moment, on the ice, Lian was performing her
compulsory spiral sequence. Left leg up in the air, arms out
to her side, fists opening and closing in time to the music as
if doing carpal-tunnel therapy exercises, she sailed right in

front of the announcer's booth, smiling beatifically. When
Lian heard Jordan's name, however, the beatific smile wa-
vered. She snapped her head to one side, glaring at Francis
with disapproval and just a touch of confusion—as if she
sincerely didn't grasp why anyone would be talking about
the inferior Jordan while the obviously superior Lian was on
the ice. Francis caught her gaze and they locked eyes for a
beat. Point made, Lian went back to her smile. Her fury, as
far as Bex noticed, was the single, genuinely emotional moment of the entire program.

Lian was taking her bows and furrowing her brow at the
Russians in the audience, who were already starting to clap
for Galina waiting in the wings, when Francis continued, "It
is ironic that Igor's death, which happened right here in
Moscow, just this past week, came at a time when the rivalry
between his student, Jordan Ares, and Gary Gold's student,
Lian Reilly, is reaching a peak as feverish as the one reached
over twenty years earlier by Gary and Igor themselves!"

"Don't be ridiculous, Francis!" Diana interjected as Brittany Monroe, seemingly still wincing from a pain of indeterminate origin, stepped onto the ice. The Russians, who
had been clapping in anticipation of Galina being the next
skater, abruptly stopped their cheers and commenced talking
amongst themselves. Suddenly, Bex believed she could see
the origin of Brittany's wincing.

Nevertheless, the pride of Ohio bravely skated out to the
center of the ice, raising her arms in what might have been
surrender, crossing them at the wrists in what might have
been martyrdom, then splaying her fingers and pressing her
palms forward which, in conjunction with her gleaming
white dress and matching ballerina-bun scrunchie, meant
only one thing to Bex. *Swan Lake. Let the downy death
throes begin.*

And, as soon as they did, Francis and Diana whipped
through Brittany's bio: Born in Cleveland, blah, blah . . .
Russian grandfather, blah, blah, blah . . . first American ever

to represent Russia . . . great presentation . . . weak jumps . . .
oops, here she goes popping her combination now—so that
they could get to the good stuff.

Francis intoned, "The Lian Reilly and Jordan Ares rivalry
is every bit as exciting as the one between their respective
coaches, Gary Gold and Igor Marchenko, who tragically
died earlier this week inside this very arena."

"Nonsense. Gary Gold was the defending United States
senior men's champion in 1978, and Igor Marchenko was
the World Bronze Medalist when they went head-to-head for
the first time as Americans. That was a much greater clash
of the Titans than Jordan and Ares. Why, neither girl has yet
to win a National, much less an international title!"

"Exactly," Francis agreed. Then promptly disagreed.
"Igor was quite clearly the superior skater of the two. Gary
never succeeded in beating him on the international stage. In
1977, when Igor won his World Bronze Medal, Gary only
finished in eleventh place. There was no reason to think he
could beat Igor domestically, and he never did, not once
when they were competing against each other."

Since this was a fact Bex had actually written down for
him—in three different places, to make sure he saw it eventually—Francis turned to her as he said it, winking at Bex as
if he'd done her a favor by indulging her little hobby and actually including some of her research in the broadcast. She
smiled back and nodded encouragingly, hoping the positive
feedback might prompt him to do it more often.

"Exactly," Diana agreed to disagree. "Jordan and Lian are
much more evenly matched than Igor and Gary. Whenever
Igor and Gary went head-to-head, we always knew who
would win in advance. Jordan and Lian are two undefeated
gladiators entering the great coliseum. We can only guess
which one will step out alive!"

All they knew for sure was that it wouldn't be Brittany
Monroe. Her program, due to the popped combination,
ended up scoring lower than Lian's. She slunk off the ice,

looking like she was going to cry. Bex felt duly bad about her downy death crack earlier, no matter how prophetic it turned out to be.

Galina Semenova took to the ice several minutes later wearing a flowing white peasant blouse and a red skirt, both embroidered with matching flower patterns to suggest a traditional Russian folk costume. Even before Galina's music commenced playing, Bex began to quietly—and sarcastically—hum "Kalinka," a traditional Russian folk melody. She had barely gotten through the first verse when the sound system at the arena joined her. Bex didn't think she was being obnoxious, just experienced. When ice-dancers wore Russian peasant costumes it was because they were skating to the (actually Gypsy) "Two Guitars." When Pairs did it, it was because they'd chosen the (actually Jewish-American) *Fiddler on the Roof.* For men, the costume meant "Volga Boatmen" and for women, it was inevitably, "Kalinka."

Galina's short program also started with some rhythmic ice-tapping, only in this case, unlike Lian who'd smacked it with the flat of her blade to indicate her tempestuous character, Galina dug in with the *back* of her blade, knee straight, arms pointing proudly towards her upturned toe, to indicate her wholesome folksiness.

Francis and Diana watched the cultural display without uttering a word beyond her name. Then, Galina got down to what she did best: a triple Lutz/triple Loop combination that barely left the ground but whipped around with such speed that it seemed like her carroty curls were twirling a beat behind each revolution and actually landed after she did.

Francis said, "A gladiator, Diana, is an athlete at the ultimate peak of his condition. It is something that Igor and Gary already were in 1978 and for the four years they were competing against each other. Lian and Jordan are most certainly not at this point, at their peak. These two young women are still developing their styles. They are not gladiators. They are not soup. These are, at best, sous-chefs."

Galina's scores came up on the electric board over their heads, indicating that she was ahead of Lian and Brittany for this phase of the competition. When such a travesty happened, a foreigner ahead of an American, the protocol was to promptly ignore Lian—now that she wasn't going to win, at least tonight; she was, in Gil's words, "dead." Instead, the focus would be on which American still could best Galina, which, in this case, was Jordan, who hadn't even skated yet.

As they went to commercial break, Francis dutifully posed this question to the folks at home: "Jordan Ares—will she be able to win it all, or will the recent death of her coach, Igor Marchenko, who was brutally murdered earlier this week in this very arena, unhinge Jordan enough to allow Galina Semenova to sneak ahead?"

In a few minutes, they had their answer.

Nope. Not Jordan.

If there was anything capable of unhinging Jordan, apparently having her coach collapse and die at her feet (right here in this very arena—had you heard?) wasn't it.

She skated her short program to the ska-ish music of No Doubt in a hot pink dress and matching boots; her blond hair combed off her face by a neat, French braid. Jordan landed a triple Lutz/double-Loop combination. Galina may have done a triple-triple, but Jordan made up for her one less revolution in the combination with the hang-time she achieved during both jumps.

As Jordan dove, headfirst, into her combination Flying Camel/Windmill spin, Diana said, "She certainly is a spectacular competitor. If this is what you call a skating souschef, Francis, I'd love to know your definition of what a full meal might be!"

Bex was about to scribble Diana a note suggesting she was mixing her metaphors when, over the headset, Gil pumped, "That's telling him! You go, go, girl! Keep up the chatter. Keep it up! Nothing more boring than a chick on the ice skating to silence."

This time, Bex didn't even consider bothering to write Gil a little note correcting him; technically speaking, the "chicks" weren't skating to silence. They did have music playing. Granted, when the skater in question was Galina it was a bit hard to discern but, sometimes, ideally even, the skaters coordinated their movements to said music.

And Diana and Francis chattering blithely over it did make those rare moments of choreography even harder to spot.

Listening closely to every single word Francis and Diana uttered on the air to ensure that they didn't say anything libelous, slanderous, or simply plain wrong, made it difficult for Bex to process those words for any significance beyond the immediate. So it wasn't until after the broadcast was over (final standings: Jordan in first place, Galina in second, Lian third, and Brittany fourth), when Bex and Sasha were lugging the research binders from the announcer's booth back to the underground offices, that Bex remembered to ask Sasha: "The pin that we found in Igor Marchenko's hotel room—the U.S. World Team pin—it said 1977, didn't it?"

Bex set her research binder down in the middle of the hallway, not caring that the middle pages ended up awkwardly folded when it tipped over. She dug into her coat pocket, looking for the pin.

But, even before she'd found it and confirmed that the date was, indeed, 1977, Sasha remembered, "You said 1977 is the year when Igor defects. So it is the year of his first American World Team."

Bex shook her head and said, "Yes," feeling a bit like Francis with his ability to contradict his own self, then added, "He did defect in 1977, that's right. But he defected after the World Championships. Well, actually right *at* the World Championships. The ones where he won a Bronze Medal. That was 1977. Francis and Diana both said so. So he couldn't have been a member of the 1977 U.S. World Team. This pin can't be his."

"Does this matter?" Sasha asked.

"I don't know," Bex admitted. "But if it's not his pin, whose pin is it? And why does he have it?"

"Perhaps he is good friends with somebody who is on the American World Team in 1977," Sasha suggested.

"Perhaps," Bex agreed. And then she added, "You know who might have the answer to that question? The only 1977 U.S. World Team member currently in Moscow. Gary Gold."

Fifteen

𝐵ex questioned Gary in her usual, low-key manner.

She thrust the pin in front of him and asked, "Do you know what this is?"

She'd ambushed Gary as he was exiting the hotel restaurant Moscow Nights. Upon spotting him through the window, sifting there alone, peacefully chewing his Chicken Kiev and drinking a glass of white wine, dressed, like always, in a freshly pressed, dark suit and dapper yet subdued tie, wiping each corner of his mouth with two, gentle taps after each bite and/or sip, Bex's first instinct was to burst right in, grab the seat across from him, and talk turkey . . . er . . . Chicken Kiev. But there was something unapproachable about Gary. It wasn't that he was frightening, like Valeri Konstantin, or weird, like Lian Reilly, or even inscrutable, like Jordan Ares. Gary was simply . . . serene. You not only couldn't rock his boat, you didn't even want to. Bex imagined that all Gary had to do was simply point his tranquil gaze at an interloper, and said interloper would fly backwards, as if hit by a mighty wind. His equanimity was that impossible to breech.

And so Bex fought her urge to tackle him at the table. She was very impressed by her newfound maturity.

That lasted only as long as it took Gary to finish his dinner.

As soon as he was out the door, Bex was out of patience. Telling Sasha to play interference with anyone who might think to interrupt her stalking session, Bex planted herself in Gary's path. And showed him the pin.

Gary took it out of her hand, holding the quarter-sized object up to the light for a better view. He held the golden pin between his thumb and forefinger, examining the back, examining the front, before handing it back to Bex.

And then he asked, "Have I suffered a head injury, Miss Levy?"

The question was so odd, Bex felt grateful for the couple who, at that moment, came out of the restaurant door and were forced to step between her and Gary. It blocked Bex's view of Gary. But, it also blocked his view of her. Which was good. Because she didn't need him seeing her looking totally stymied. That would be unprofessional.

Finally, Bex gave up. Allowing Gary to be courteous and lead her away from the door so as not to impair anyone else's passing, Bex paused under a fake fir tree, festively decorated with glass balls, silver tinsel, and tiny Santa Claus puppets—not for Christmas, but for the Russian New Year. Which bore a striking resemblance to the Christmas that had been outlawed under the Communists (religion, Karl Marx warned, was an opiate of the masses).

Bex said, "I'm sorry, Gary. I don't understand your question."

"You asked me whether I knew what the object in your hand was. It is clearly a pin from the 1977 United States World Figure Skating Team. Since that is obvious from the fact that the words: 1977 U.S. Figure Skating Team are emblazoned upon its front, I can only assume that this is either a trick question, or that I have recently bumped my head and you are trying to ascertain whether or not I am cognizant."

Bex said, "You're overthinking this."

"Perhaps it is you who would like some time to rethink your question."

They were in a fairly isolated corner of the hotel lobby, shielded by the restaurant door on one side, and the fake fir, complete with cotton mounds of snow, on the other. The only people Bex could imagine approaching them at this time of night were lost drunks or Santa. And Sasha had orders to shoot either of those on sight.

So she felt safe asking Gary, "Do you have any idea whom this pin belongs to?"

"Igor," he said without a moment's hesitation. "Or, at least it belonged to him in the past. I saw him wear it numerous times to competitions, on his lapel. He called it his good-luck charm."

"But, it's a 1977 U.S. World Team pin."

"Once again, Miss Levy, I refer you to the fact that such information is clearly printed on the front. You are not making any earth-shaking discoveries, I am afraid."

"Igor"—Bex tried to keep her temper in check—"did not become a member of the U.S .World Team until 1978; he defected at the 1977 Worlds. This pin can't be his. I mean, it couldn't have been his, originally."

"That is correct."

"So my question is, do you know whose pin this was, before Igor got it?"

"Yes, I do."

"Do you feel like telling me, maybe?" Bex was practically jumping up and down now, crunching the cottony snow and causing the ornaments to shake nervously.

Gary sighed. He looked Bex in the eyes. And he said, "The pin was once mine."

Bex stared right back at him. It was the only thing she

could think of to do. Well, actually it was one of two things. The other was to blurt out, "Say what?"

"The pin was once mine," he repeated, just as calmly. "I gave it to Igor once." He paused, reconsidered. "No. That is not precisely true."

"You mean he stole it from you?"

"Igor Marchenko"—Gary pronounced each syllable with great care—"stole my professional career. My national title. My chance for an Olympic medal, and money that should have gone to support an American skater. But, no. He did not steal my pin."

"Then how did he get it?"

Gary sighed again. Bex wondered if she was boring him. He asked, "Were you even alive in 1977, Miss Levy?"

Bex shook her head, feeling guilty, though she wasn't sure for what.

"In 1977, I wouldn't say that the Cold War was at its zenith—that may have been the 1950s, when everyone expected nuclear war to come at any second—but, in 1977, the Cold War was certainly at a pressure point. The Soviets had endured several very high profile, very embarrassing defections. Nureyev in 1961, Stalin's own daughter in 1967, Baryshnikov in 1974. They were . . . unusually . . . eager to prevent history from repeating itself. To that end, all of the Soviet skaters at the 1977 World Championships were watched every minute of every day. And night. Their coaches and team leaders, if they were not actual KGB members, were at the very least, informers. They reported on the athletes because they knew it was their own future on the line, should anything inappropriate occur. Igor's coach, Alexandr Troika was his name, took the directive to contain his skater, I believe, a bit more to heart than most. It was freezing in Moscow that February. Well, I suppose it is freezing in Moscow every February, but I can only speak to the ones I have personally experienced. Naturally, the skaters' hotel had no heat. I understand that was par for the

course, then. The maintenance staff kept promising us it
would be fixed soon. It was never fixed. We spoiled Americans slept under specially imported blankets and in our
team's uniform parkas to keep warm. Igor, on the other
hand . . . Igor's coach wanted to make sure that Igor would
not go outside unsupervised. So he locked away Igor's
jacket, his boots, his gloves, his hat, even his street shoes.
He left him one pair of sweatpants, a T-shirt, and bedroom
slippers. In a Moscow winter, in a hotel with no heat, that
was all he allowed Igor to have."

"Wasn't he afraid of Igor getting sick before the competition?"

"It was not his chief concern," Gary replied. And then,
without any sort of shift in his tone, he, just as matter-of-
factly told Bex, "But I could not allow Igor to go out into the
street like that. He was willing to. He was that eager to defect. But, I could not let him do it. I gave him my jacket. Not
the team jacket; he would be too quickly recognized as not
belonging. But I gave him my own jacket that I had brought,
just in case. I gave him my boots, my gloves, my scarf, my
socks. Otherwise, I was certain he would freeze to death before reaching the American embassy."

Bex couldn't believe what she was hearing. "You? You
were the one who helped Igor Marchenko escape the hotel?"

"I merely loaned him some warm clothes. Igor was the
one who dared to stuff himself down the garbage disposal
and onto the street."

"You never said a word about it! Neither did he!"

"What was there to say?"

"All those years the press was writing about you two
being rivals—"

"We were rivals."

"But you saved his life!"

"And what should that matter? We were rivals for the
U.S. Championship. Everything else was an irrelevant detail."

"You always said you thought the USFSA shouldn't have supported Igor, especially not financially. You signed a petition to Congress to keep him from getting his citizenship. But you're the one who facilitated his defection. If you hadn't helped Igor, he might have never come to the U.S. He might have never taken your career."

"That, too, is an irrelevant detail."

"Is it because you didn't think he'd be allowed to skate in U.S.? Is that why you helped him? Because you didn't expect him to take your place?"

"I did not think about it." Gary was peering at Bex as if she were particularly and uniquely dense. "I saw a person who desperately needed help. Whose life was in literal danger. I did not think about whether I liked him or not. I did not think about what might happen to me down the line if I helped him. I certainly did not think about skating. All I did was—"

She understood.

She said, "All you did was grab Igor by the back of the collar and hide him under the bed until the Nazis left the courtyard. . . ."

Gary stopped peering at Bex as if she were particularly dense. He nodded. And then he even smiled.

"Yes," he said. "I am not a Nazi, Miss Levy. Which is more than can be said for that coach of Igor's. Taking away his clothes was only the tip of that particular iceberg. The night of the men's long program, after Igor had won the Bronze medal, I walked into the men's bathroom at the arena, and I watched Troika beating Igor with his own medal. It was solid. It was heavy. And he was hitting Igor about the face and neck, hard enough to leave black and blue bruises. He was screaming that Igor had not skated the best he was capable of. That he deliberately disgraced the motherland. Igor was taking it all, too. Until I walked in. A teenage boy can put up with a lot of abuse. But not when another teenage boy is there to see it. Igor was so embarrassed to have me witness his humiliation, that he began screaming at Troika, fighting back. I did not understand what he said, they were shouting in Russian, but I certainly understand what Igor was trying to convey when he took his Bronze medal and flung it into the toilet."

Bex already knew this part of the story, courtesy of Shura's earlier, "Shit! Shit! Shit!" denunciation. But she still gasped.

Gary said, "I thought Troika was going to kill him then. He had his fingers about Igor's throat and he was banging his head against the bathroom stall. I had to pull Troika off him. I screamed that I would get the ISU officials, and that calmed him down. Or at least brought him to his senses. He left the bathroom, still screaming at Igor. That was when I offered Igor my coat and my boots. Because this was no longer some abstract, political cause. It was a true matter of life and death.

"Oh." Gary chuckled. "And I also encouraged Igor to fish his medal out of the toilet and take it with him. Troika or not, it was still a great achievement to win a Bronze medal at the World Championship. I told him he would want to have it someday. And now . . . now that Bronze medal hangs in the USFSA museum, right next to the Gold Igor won for America at the Olympics, and the three National titles he won from me. Ironic, isn't it?"

Bex didn't know what to say. She really only had one more question. "The pin?"

"Yes?"

"How did Igor get your pin?"

"Oh, that." Gary waved the question away as not being worth the discussion. "It was in the pocket of my jacket. I did not remember that when I gave it to him. He wore it as a good luck charm. Though, once, he did ask me if I wanted it back." Gary smiled again at Bex. "I told him to keep it. After all, 1977 proved a much luckier year for him in the end than it did for me, wouldn't you say?"

Sixteen

Bex said to Sasha, "If my life were easy, that pin with the wrong date on it should have led me to Igor's killer. Leopold and Loeb, you know, they were caught because one of them dropped his eyeglasses at the murder site. Why couldn't this have been the same deal? It would have been so perfect! And, most importantly, it would have been over!"

They were sitting on a leather couch in the hotel lobby. On either side of them, women in miniskirts, floor-length fur coats and knee-high boots held hands with men dressed in suits that wouldn't have looked out of place in a *Guys and Dolls* revival as they left the hotel restaurant and headed out the door into the snow, ready to begin the post-midnight portion of their partying. Bex rested her chin on her hands, nibbled her index fingernail, spit it out, then took a deep breath. She was in the process of fantasizing about a few blissful hours of bedridden unconsciousness, during which she wouldn't have to worry about homeopathic poisons, homicidal teammates, bickering announcers, wannabe Russians, screaming producers, and/or misplaced World Team pins, when Sasha offered, "We should to go out."

Already in the process of turning another nail into a midnight supper, Bex had to cough and clear her mouth before she asked, "What?"

"We have been working very hard. There is no more work to do tonight. Come, I invite you to come with me. There is a club for dancing, it is only around the corner. We will go out now. Come."

"Come" was not what Bex wanted to do right now. "Go" had been more her train of thought. She looked at Sasha. He was sitting up straight, hair tousled from the hat he'd been pulling on and off all day. His eyes were shining and he was grinning; the left side of his smile rising just a fraction higher than the right for a lopsided, mischievous effect. He held out one hand to Bex.

She took it.

The club was called *Ridiska*. Which, Sasha explained, was street-slang for "a bad sort of person, like a thief or maybe criminal." It also, he admitted, literally meant "radish." As in the little red root vegetable. Bex laughed. Sasha laughed with her and gallantly removed her parka, handing it to the coat-check girl. Which was when Bex got her first clue that she was a tad underdressed for the establishment.

The miniskirts, maxi-boots and floor-length furs had all, apparently, been headed this way. So had the glittery earrings that dripped from lobes to shoulders, the necklaces that splayed across a procession of well-endowed—probably enhanced—chests like so many affluent-pointing arrows, and the rings with stones so illuminated they could be used to send desperate bat-signals across the night sky.

Bex, for her part, was wearing jeans (the same ones that not so long ago had been brushing along the sludge in the refrigeration room), a black turtleneck sweater, because black didn't show as much dirt and/or sweat as a more primary color might have, and a 24/7 yellow fleece jacket that she was actually using as a second layer sweater. Oh, yes, and sneakers. Can't forget about the sneakers. Or the brown, wool tights under the jeans.

So not only was she not in fashion, she was also very hot.

Because the club itself, in contrast with the Moscow winter, was sweltering.

And very, very noisy.

A band in the corner, wedged between the dance floor and the dining area, was playing something . . . uh . . . loud. A male lead singer and three female backup ones were attempting to shout over the din of their two guitars, electrical organ, and drum set. They must have been doing a pretty decent job because, after not even really listening for a minute or two, Bex was able to figure out that they weren't, as she'd first assumed, singing in Russian, but rather attempting to howl through a "re-imagining" of "I Can't Get No Satisfaction" before segueing into a no less energetically Slavic, "Yesterday." In Russia, Bex guessed, the year was perennially 1965.

Sasha gestured for Bex to follow him, and she did, trying to ignore the hot lights that were pointing at the disco ball in the center of the dance floor. The frozen core she'd acquired over a full season at the skating rink quickly began to melt. Soon, Bex's cheeks flamed crimson, and her armpits opened the sweaty floodgates. It could not possibly be a good sign when you could not only feel the perspiration dripping down your sides, between your breasts and down your chin, but also from your eyelashes and teeth, as well.

Sasha led Bex to the center of the dance floor. All around them, the *Guys and Dolls* public either barely swayed their upper bodies in an attempt to appear perennially cool (and perhaps not risk losing either their jewelry or their natty fedoras) even while dancing, or went whole hog in the other direction, sacrificing cool for acrobatic, with the men hitting the floor in showy splits, then sliding up again with no hand support. Their women, meanwhile, were kicking up their knees and the fronts of their dresses, throwing their heads back and parading from one end of the floor to the other, shaking their hips and clicking their heels for good measure, yippee-ya-yaying. To be honest, Bex wasn't sure which exhibition she was hoping Sasha might favor her with. All she knew was, she personally was in no shape to be trying either.

Fortunately, she didn't have to. Sasha just looked around them, shrugged with a "What can you do?" smile, and held out his arms, waiting for Bex to step into them.

She did.

It would have been impolite not to.

He was stronger, more solid than he seemed. The skinny frame was misleading. Sasha may have been thin, but he was also coated in muscle. It made whatever belief Bex still harbored of his being a "boy," disappear. This was no boy. This was a man.

He didn't say anything while they danced, the music taking a leap forward from 1965 to the next decade, as the group launched into their ode to disco. Bex probably could not have heard Sasha even if he had tried to say anything, but the fact that he didn't feel compelled to make idle chatter somehow made him seem even more adult.

Somewhere in the middle of "Last Dance," they both turned their heads at the same time, and ended up face-to-face. Again. Bex felt herself flushing hotter, as even her elbows joined the sweaty limb parade. Sasha didn't seem perturbed at all. Instead, he looked as if he'd been expecting it. Not hoping for, but patiently expecting, all along.

He leaned over and kissed Bex on the lips. Gently, politely, but not at all shyly. And then he leaned back. And waited for her to make the next move.

What a shame Bex had no next move to make.

She felt she should definitely say something now. But she knew she wouldn't be heard. She felt she should do something to indicate how she felt about the kiss. She did wish she knew how she felt about the kiss.

She stopped dancing. Not by choice, she was just rooted to the ground. Like a radish. She turned around and headed out of the club. It was only when she'd pushed her way through the dancing crowd to the door that Bex thought it might have been helpful if she'd gestured for Sasha to follow her. Because she did want him to follow her. At least, she thought she did.

She could no longer see him.

She wondered if he thought she'd run away.

She wondered if she had run away.

She stood outside the door to the club, on the street, without her coat. How very Cinderella-ish. Only instead of leaving a glass slipper behind, she'd left her bulky parka. Who said life wasn't a fairy tale?

Sasha said, "You are angry, again."

He'd come out, also without a coat, and stood behind her.

"No," Bex denied automatically, even before she'd fully processed his question. "I'm not angry. Not now."

"You were angry with me before. I did not understand why."

"You mean when you told me about how Russians lie about everything?"

"Yes."

"It's very confusing."

"I am sorry."

"I mean, how am I supposed to know when you're lying and when you're telling the truth. You just kissed me right now. Does that mean you like me, or are you, I don't know, using me for something, like you said all Russians do?"

"I like you, Bex," he said.

"And I'm just supposed to believe you?"

Sasha shrugged. "I am sorry it is so confusing for you. I am not confused."

"Shurik!" A male voice calling from across the street

prompted both of them to turn their heads. Bex because it was a welcome, piercing noise to distract from the uncomfortable silence, and Sasha because the holler had apparently been for him.

A young man about Sasha's age ducked around three angry, honking cars to jog across the street and sweep Sasha into a bear hug, followed by a manly kiss on both cheeks. They chatted gleefully in Russian, with Sasha pointing once in Bex's direction and the other young man nodding approvingly. At least, Bex hoped it was approvingly. She didn't know who this guy was or what they were talking about. But she still wanted the tacit approval. She was pretty needy that way.

After a few minutes, the pair slapped each other heartily on the back, more manly kissing, and then the new guy disappeared into the bowels of the club. With one more—approving?—glance at Bex.

She asked, "Who was that?"

"Old friend," Sasha said. "From my orphanage. We were youths together. We played on the same soccer team. It is very good to see him. Very good. So many boys from my orphanage, their lives, they are not so good. No work. No hope. Not like me. I am fortunate. I have ambition. A dream. This is important."

Bex asked, "He didn't call you Sasha. He called you something else."

"Shurik." Sasha nodded his head. "That is what they called me in orphanage. It is name my father called me. After I am graduated, I do not want to be that person. I do not want to be poor, sad, little Shurik with no parents, anymore. So I change my name. I am Sasha. Sasha is new name for new life."

"Did you have to change it legally?" Bex couldn't believe the two of them were actually having a calm discussion about Russia's identity laws. But she guessed it beat babbling incoherently, which was her only other alternative.

"Oh, no. No. Because I do not change my name written in my passport. Sasha is just nickname. I simply to change my nickname, this is allowed. Like Bex is nickname for Rebecca, and Fedya for Fedor, Sasha is nickname for Alexander."

Bex froze. And this time, it had nothing to do with the weather or the season or her lack of parka. It didn't even have to do with her trying to avoid talking about what had just happened between them.

Slowly, she repeated, "Sasha is a nickname for Alexander?"

"Yes. It is."

"And that other name he called you—"

"Shurik?"

"Yes, Shurik. That's a nickname for Alexander, too?"

"Yes."

Bex grabbed Sasha's hand, squeezing his fingers and practically hopping up and down with excitement. "Sasha!" she exclaimed. "I know who killed Igor Marchenko!"

Seventeen

Sasha was right there with her. Whatever he'd been thinking about or planning for earlier seemingly went out the window when confronted with Bex's enthusiasm. He allowed her to keep hopping as he clutched her hand and asked, equally pumped, "Who?"

She stopped jumping. She said, "I just have to make one phone call, first."

They barely paused to retrieve their jackets from the coat-check before rushing back to Bex's hotel room. Bex was feeling so awesome she even managed a smile and a cheery wave for their floor matron. The woman just stared at her suspiciously.

Bex had her fingers on the phone's touch pad as soon as she crossed the threshold, leaving Sasha to close her door behind them. She dialed the number from memory, and, because of the time difference with Colorado Springs, Colorado, was happy to get an answer on the second ring. Bex asked her question. Sasha, listening, cocked his head in surprise. She made a gesture with her arm that Bex hoped translated as, "Trust me."

"Are you sure?" Bex asked the U.S. Figure Skating Association Museum's curator. "Yeah, why don't you go ahead and double-check. I'll hold."

Seeing that Bex was just waiting, Sasha started to ask a question. Bex shook her head. This was too good. She didn't want to break the spell.

"It is there?" Bex sighed with relief "Great. Thank you. Thank you so much!"

She hung up the phone and turned back to Sasha, grinning. She might have begun hopping up and down again if she weren't sitting on her bed at a most uncomfortable angle. She also might have taken a moment to feel embarrassed that Sasha was seeing her hotel room in all its unkempt glory, including the clothes she'd worn yesterday lying in a heap on a chair in the corner and her T-shirt nightgown crumpled at the foot of the bed. But, Bex had no time for such pettiness now.

She told Sasha, "Igor Marchenko's World Bronze medal is hanging at the USFSA museum, just like Gary Gold said it was!"

Sasha nodded. He peeled off his jacket as well as the sweater underneath and took a seat next to Bex on the bed. He courteously pretended not to notice the balled up T-shirt nightgown. He said, "And this is evidence pointing at who killed Marchenko?"

"Sort of," Bex said. "Gary Gold told me the night Igor defected, he was so angry at his coach, he threw his Bronze medal in the toilet."

"Yes, that is why Shura said Russians are so angry with Igor. Because he insulted his country and his people."

"But how did Shura know that? The medal didn't stay in the toilet. It's hanging in the USFSA Museum. And I've read a ton of press about Igor's defection. No one ever mentioned that detail. So the only people who knew what Igor did were Igor, Gary, and his coach, Alexandr Troika."

"Alexandr Troika." As soon as Bex spelled it out for him, Sasha saw where she was going. That seemed to be another thing they had in common. "Alexandr. Shura."

"Yes!" Bex wanted to throw her arms around him and kiss him. And some of it was even because she was really happy about figuring out who killed Igor. "Shura, the arena manger, has got to be the coach, Alexandr Troika. How else would he know about Igor's medal?"

"Perhaps Alexandr Troika told him? Or Alexandr Troika told Konstantin and he told Shura, or—"

Bex said, "I have to make one more phone call."

This time, she had to look up the phone number. And this time, without the time difference, the person on the other end wasn't nearly as gracious about hearing from her at two A.M. He did, however, grudgingly, give Bex the answer she needed.

She hung up and told Sasha, "It doesn't matter who told whom what about Igor's medal being thrown in the toilet. Shura is definitely Alexandr Troika. Konstantin claims he didn't tell me that before because he assumed I knew about it. And because I didn't ask." This was often the biggest problem in her investigations. Not so much that Bex got the wrong answers, but that she forgot to ask the right questions.

"Shura is Alexandr Troika," Sasha agreed. "How does this prove he is the killer of Igor Marchenko?"

Bex sighed. And got ready to make some more phone calls.

By breakfast the next morning—Bex was very proud of herself for having waited until all of six A.M. before she commenced dialing—Bex had accumulated several more answers to advance her theory.

Sveta and Luba confirmed that while the threatening voice on the phone told them he was Valeri Konstantin, they had no actual proof that it was, in fact, Konstantin calling. Neither had spoken to the man in years, so they didn't remember too clearly what his voice sounded like. So, yes, in theory, it could have been Troika on the phone, pretending to be Konstantin in order to keep the two women away from the arena, where they might have seen him and recognized Igor's former coach as their more recent tormenter. It made sense that, if Shura were plotting to kill Igor, he wouldn't want anyone around who could point him out to the victim in advance.

Bex's next stop was back out on the street with Fedya the knife-wielder. When she asked him if Shura might have bought some digitalis from him, Fedya nodded. "Of course. He buys from me regularly. A bad heart, he has."

"Why didn't you tell me this before, when I wanted to know if anybody from the arena had bought digitalis prior to Marchenko's death?"

Fedya replied, "You asked me if any new people, from the skating competition, buy from me. You did not ask about people who buy regularly. I told you, I have many regular clients inside the arena."

And so he had.

Bex thanked Fedya. And she told Sasha over breakfast in the hotel dining room, "He's our man, I'm sure of it."

"So what is then the next step?"

Bex said, "We go to the police with what we've found out. We tell them that a man who had threatened to kill Igor Marchenko on several occasions purchased the drug used to kill him a few days before his death. Even in Russia, that ought to be enough to have him brought in for questioning, oughtn't it?"

"I believe this, yes."

Bex grinned, imagining how Gil would be forced to grudgingly—and publicly—compliment her, as she wondered, "What do you think is the best time of day to contact the police so that they come arrest Shura during the long program broadcast tonight?"

Sasha asked, "This will be big story on the news, then?"

"Oh, yes. I definitely think so. I mean, do you remember all the press that was here the first day? This will get a lot of play. Not just in Russia, all over the world. Gil is going to love me for this. This is guaranteed ratings gold!"

Sasha said, "Bex . . ."

"What?" She may have ostensibly been having this conversation with him but, in all honesty, Bex had been spinning giddily in her own world, counting her Emmy Awards before they were hatched. She hadn't noticed Sasha's growing anxiety. Which was odd in and off itself, since he always seemed so confident in whatever he was doing.

"I have to ask you, Bex, a question."

"What?" she repeated, the food in her throat turning into a cactus needle. *Why is he looking so serious? What have I missed?*

"I am asking you, please do not tell Mr. Cahill about Shura."

"Why not?"

"Because. I would like you to allow me to tell someone else."

"You mean you want to warn Shura?"

He was actually blushing. Bex didn't realize he knew how. "There is a television station. It is here, in Moscow. Many times, I have asked for position there. Many times, the boss, he has told me, no. He says I do not know enough people. I cannot to bring him important news stories before everyone else."

Now it was Bex's turn to, once again, figure out the big picture based on some clearly spelled out clues. She summarized, "You want me to let you bring this guy my exclusive, so you can get a job at his TV station."

Sasha nodded. And looked pleadingly at Bex.

She said, "Why should I believe you?"

He blinked. "I do not understand. You do not believe me?"

"Oh, I believe you know a guy who promised you a TV job if you can get him an exclusive about Marchenko. I'm sure that part is true. What I mean is, how do I know this hasn't been your plan all along?"

"But . . ." Sasha stammered. "This *has* been my plan all along."

Well, he had her there. It was pretty hard to remain accusatory and self-righteous when your subject was confirming all the accusations.

Sasha reminded, "I tell you this, first day we are meeting. I tell you I desire to find employment in television."

And so he had. "But you didn't tell me you intended to use me to do it!"

"Yes, I did," he insisted.

She was getting a headache.

Amazing how Bex could spend days sifting through lies, and lies to cover up lies, and lies about things no one had any good reason to be lying about, all the while keeping her head clear and focused on the task at hand. Ten minutes of talking to Sasha, and Bex felt like her brain was having a coughing fit.

She asked, "Why should I do this for you?"

"Because. You are nice person."

"I'll be a nice person without a job if Gil ever finds out. Big story exclusives are all he cares about. Maybe this will make your career, but it will ruin mine."

"I realize this," Sasha said. And yet he didn't look like he planned to withdraw his request anytime soon.

"Is that why you kissed me?" Bex figured she might as well ask exactly what was on her mind. Especially since

that question was so dominant, her mind was proving incapable of coming up with any other query to push the former
back into queue.

"No." Sasha did not hesitate.

"Are you telling the truth?"

He didn't reply.

He simply smiled.

Epilogue

The arrest came at five P.M. local time. Too early for 24/7's broadcast, but just in time to be the lead, live story on the Moscow news.

Shura didn't deny a thing. The last Bex saw of him, he was ranting in Russian to no one in particular as he was shoved into the back of a police car, the on-the-spot camera crew pushing its way through the gathering crowd to record every word. Bex saw Sasha in the crowd. He was standing a few feet behind the camera, right next to a man Bex guessed was the segment's producer. They both looked very happy.

Gil Cahill, however, did not.

He came out as soon as a sycophantic production assistant gave him a heads-up about the excitement. He headed straight for Bex.

"What the hell is going on here, Miss Crack-Shot Researcher?"

"The arena manager is being arrested for the murder of Igor Marchenko. Turns out he's Igor's old coach. Alexandr

Troika, a.k.a. Shura, never forgave Igor for defecting and ruining his life. He was forbidden from coaching, demoted to
working as a janitor at the same arena where he'd once
trained champions. It took him twenty years just to work his
way up to arena manager, but even that was hardly what he
once expected to do with his life. So, when Shura finally got
his chance, he poisoned Marchenko. He tried to pin the
blame on Gary, claiming he saw Gary with Igor's gloves.
Gary, by the way, isn't one of Shura's favorite people, either.
But it was Shura all along."

"And why the hell is this story going exclusive to some
nothing Russian network instead of the one that's, at least
for now, paying your salary?"

"Well, see, that's a funny story, Gil." Bex took a step back
so that they might have a better view of the rooftop on the
building directly across the street from the arena. "Turns
out, by a weird coincidence, one of our 24/7 crews was up
on the roof, shooting the beautiful Moscow scenery. They
got the whole thing, from the police car coming up, to Shura
being led out in handcuffs, to his on-air confession. Not only
will we be the first Western outlet to have this story, but
we'll also have it from a camera angle no one else has, so it
will look totally different. Pretty lucky for us, isn't it?"

Gil stared at Bex for what felt like an eternity. She stared
back, smiling sweetly. It was a trick she'd recently picked up
from a close friend.

Finally, Gil grunted, "Beginner's luck, kid. Dumb, old
beginner's luck."

And then he went inside to call the network and let them
know about his foresight in putting a camera crew up on the
roof to insure their exclusive.

The hubbub was dying down. Sasha looked over the
crowd and met Bex's eyes.

He blew her a kiss.

She kept smiling.

**Judging figure skating can be
ice-cold murder.**

Murder on Ice
A Figure Skating Mystery Series
by Alina Adams

When an Olympic judge is murdered,
it is up to figure skating researcher
Bex Levy to solve the crime before
the trail turns cold.

"ALINA ADAMS NAILS THE TRIPLE AXEL."
—MYSTERY READER

0-425-19307-1

And look for the next book in the series,
On Thin Ice
0-425-19884-7

pc597